THE DAY THE SKI LIFTS STOPPED

Downhill racers, figure skaters, millionaires, beautiful people . . . They've all gathered at SkiHaven for the winter games. They are competing on the slopes and in their beds, totally unaware they're on the brink of high altitude disaster.

AVALANCHE

A million kilos of deadly white snow— exploding across the pages in a thundering, bone-chilling superthriller of man against nature.

ROCK HUDSON   MIA FARROW

AVALANCHE

also starring
Robert Forster   Jeanette Nolan
Barry Primus   Rick Moses
Steve Franken

A New World Pictures Release

Produced by
ROGER CORMAN

AVALANCHE

Robert Weverka

Based on the Screenplay by Claude Pola

BANTAM BOOKS · TORONTO · NEW YORK · LONDON

AVALANCHE
A Bantam Book / August 1978

ISBN 0–553–12302–5

Published simultaneously in the United States and Canada

Bantam Books are published by Bantam Books, Inc. Its trade-
mark, consisting of the words "Bantam Books" and the por-
trayal of a bantam, is registered in the United States Patent
Office and in other countries. Marca Registrada. Bantam
Books, Inc., 666 Fifth Avenue, New York, New York 10019.

PRINTED IN THE UNITED STATES OF AMERICA

AVALANCHE

1

<><><><><><><><><><><><><><><><><><><><><><><><>

The drive from Cedar Falls into the Rocky Mountains was spectacular. At the lower elevations the road passed through thick forests of pines and groves of stark, leafless aspen, and there were only scattered patches of snow. Then, as they climbed higher, the ground became solid white and the pine branches began to sag under their heavy burden. By then the road was climbing sharply, and high above them the craggy white peaks and ridges soared into an incredibly blue sky.

In the back seat of the hotel taxi, Caroline Brace smiled easily to herself and tried to remember how long it had been since she had seen such dramatically beautiful scenery. A very long time, she decided, because most of her twenty-eight years had been spent in the smog-filled canyons of New York City.

She could see what must be SkiHaven Valley now, a bowl-shaped depression nestled in a semicircle of towering peaks several miles ahead of them. The driver eased his speed a little as the asphalt disappeared and they were suddenly driving in what seemed like a white trough flanked by high snowbanks.

"Did Mr. Shelby build this road?" she asked the driver.

"Yes, ma'am. It's all new, some of it blasted out of solid rock. There's an old dirt road that used to wind around over those other mountains, but this is about eight miles shorter."

Caroline smiled, knowing David would have had a great time leaning over the shoulders of the engineers and architects offering them suggestions on how to build the road. By occupation David was an investment broker, managerial expert, and builder of international conglomerates. But if a road were to be built, he wouldn't hesitate to read a dozen books on the subject and drive everybody crazy with his newfound expertise. Which was the principal reason Caroline was no longer Mrs. David Shelby.

When the plane had landed at the Cedar Glen airport thirty minutes ago, Caroline was once again reminded of his possessiveness. As quickly as she found her bags, the uniformed driver appeared at her elbow with the question "Are you Mrs. Shelby?"

"No, I'm not," she said. "My name is Caroline Brace."

The man apologized and was quickly retreating before she admitted she was the *former* Mrs. Shelby. Then she followed him out to the taxi that had the words HOTEL SIERRA

2

SERENA painted on the side. Under that in smaller lettering it said, A DAVID SHELBY ENTERPRISE.

A little more than two years had passed since she had last seen David. That was when the divorce was finalized and over cocktails at the Four Seasons restaurant he made an impassioned plea for her to forget the divorce and pick up where they had left off. The only problem was, his plea sounded very much like a sales pitch to form a conglomerate—a routine that no doubt worked very well with accountants and corporation presidents.

There was also the matter of her just having been promoted to a senior editorship at *Vogue* magazine—a problem that David brushed aside by saying she could simply quit and stay home all day. Caroline had laughed and suggested a reverse solution to the problem. He could quit working and stay home all day and she could be the breadwinner for a while. David hadn't even smiled.

Caroline still wasn't sure why she had accepted the invitation to come to Colorado for the grand opening of his new resort. Maybe it was curiosity—to see if he was still the same David. Or maybe it was just to get away for a while and have a look at the Rocky Mountains. In any case, she felt a little odd wearing boots and a parka and ski pants. The clothes were all new, and one of the other editors had assured her they were the latest thing, and she would look like she had just flown in from Switzerland. Except Caroline didn't know how to ski, and after she left Colorado she would probably never wear the clothes again.

3

The driver was slowing down again, carefully maneuvering a sharp curve before they started across a bridge.

"Did Mr. Shelby also construct the bridge?" Caroline asked.

"Yes, ma'am. That's a thousand-foot gorge down below us. Building the bridge is what saved most of the extra mileage coming up here."

Caroline ventured a hesitant look into the thousand-foot abyss, then quickly drew her head back. David must have had an even better time managing the construction of the bridge.

Once they were past the gorge they climbed through a sharp curve, and Caroline caught her first glimpse of the hotel. It was a huge, contemporary-looking mountain lodge that seemed to have a great deal of glass. A mile or so away there appeared to be a little alpine village, the quaint chalet-style buildings all heavily covered with snow. Altogether the setting was quite pretty—very much like a scene on a Christmas card.

When they finally pulled into the parking lot the driver opened the door for her, and Caroline gave the hotel a closer look while he retrieved her bags from the trunk. It was quite tastefully done; a great deal of natural rock, along with heavy timbers and glass.

Once they were up the steps and through the door, the lobby was equally impressive. Inside the starkly modern structure, the place had a warm and cozy atmosphere. Caroline smiled as she reached the reception desk. The girl behind it was about eighteen years old and was casually reading a copy of *Rolling Stone.*

"I have a reservation," Caroline said. "Caroline Brace."

The girl consulted her reservation book and frowned. "I'm sorry, I don't see it here."

Caroline smiled to herself. "Perhaps you'll find it listed as Caroline Shelby."

"Right," the girl said. "So who are you? Shelby or Brace?"

"Brace until I married Shelby. Then Brace again after we divorced. I just didn't *feel* Shelby anymore."

The girl laughed. "I'll change the reservation to Brace. Room 204."

Caroline tipped the driver, who had brought her bags in, and signed the register.

"Caroline!"

There was no mistaking the throaty feminine voice, and Caroline quickly turned. "Florence!"

David's mother was one of the few reasons Caroline regretted the divorce. She was a hard-drinking old warhorse whose only objective in life was to enjoy herself. She was also totally unimpressed by her son's accomplishments.

She was wearing a full-length mink coat over a tailored suit, which looked a little incongruous with her heavy overshoes. But Florence Shelby never paid much attention to fashions. After a bone-breaking hug, she held Caroline at arm's length.

"Did David ask you here?"

"Sure. Didn't he tell you?"

"Hah!" she snorted. "That boy never told

5

his mother anything. Except good night. Are you two getting back together?"

The question surprised Caroline. But Florence Shelby was not known for beating around the bush. "I never thought about it," Caroline said. She frowned. "Let me think about it. . . . No," she finally said.

"So why did you come? Are you some kind of masochist? God, this place is full of snow!"

"Well, let's just say I've always wanted to see the Rocky Mountains."

Mrs. Shelby's laugh echoed across the huge room and she gave Caroline another hug. "It's good to see you, sweetheart."

Caroline had scarcely noticed the bespectacled little man who had followed Mrs. Shelby across the lobby. But now he was holding up a finger as if to get Florence's attention.

"What's that?" Florence said, giving him a hard look. "Some kind of obscene proposal?"

The man seemed to be distressed about something. "Mrs. Shelby, there's a lot—"

"This person is called McDade," she said. "He works here. What did you say your job was?" she asked the man.

McDade gave Caroline a quick smile and turned back to Mrs. Shelby. "Bookkeeper. Excuse me, Mrs. Shelby, but we're supposed to be—"

"Bookkeeper," Mrs. Shelby said as if it were a distasteful word. "Not a VIP escort for the great man's mother. No offense, McDade. I like you. Some of my best friends are bookkeepers."

"Thank you," the man said. "There's a

lot I'm supposed to show you before lunch. Shall we get going?"

"Let the heart guide the head, McDade," Mrs. Shelby said. She hooked an arm into Caroline's and moved across the lobby. "Got a fella in New York?" she asked. Her elbow gave Caroline a nudge.

Caroline laughed. "Two or three."

"Jesus, are you turning into a swinger?"

"Am I? Could be. How's the great man?"

"I suppose you're referring to David S. Shelby, esquire. Right now he's up to his ass in celebrities. You want to have a look?"

Caroline didn't, but Mrs. Shelby moved her through a door to an open terrace where four or five people seemed to be holding a press conference. But David was nowhere in sight.

"There are some of the beautiful people," Florence said.

Caroline recognized the two young men who were getting most of the attention. She was not a rabid sports fan, but Bruce Scott was supposed to be America's greatest skier, and he had been on enough magazine covers that it would have been hard to miss him. Gary Buckner was equally famous—a ski jumper, as Caroline recalled. They were both in their early twenties and had the deep tans and casual self-confidence of worshiped stars.

Behind them were the two young ladies regarded as number one and two in figure-skating competition, but Caroline couldn't remember which was *one* and which was *two*.

"Aren't they beautiful?" Mrs. Shelby said wistfully.

Caroline nodded and glanced off at the girls.

"Not them," Mrs. Shelby said. "The two skiers. Now, that's a pair I wouldn't mind taking home with me."

"I don't think they'd fit in your suitcase," Caroline said.

"Don't worry, I'd find a place for them."

"After the collegiate championships," one of the reporters was saying to Gary Buckner, "you said you were leaving competition. What decided you to turn pro?"

With his flopping blond hair and pure white teeth, Buckner looked like a young Robert Redford. He flashed a smile and gave a boyish toss of his head. "I wanted to be part of this whole fantastic thing happening here. How could anyone pass up an invitation to this beautiful place?"

"May we assume Mr. Shelby made it very attractive?" another reporter asked.

"Well, he certainly helped."

There was laughter, and Bruce Scott came forward and put an arm around Buckner.

"How about you, Bruce?" someone asked. "Are we going to see the same fearless performance we saw throughout Europe this season?"

"I'll do my best for you."

"Bruce, even in your Olympic days you seemed to thrive on the riskier slopes. Have you ever known fear?"

"Known what?" Scott asked as if he had never heard the word before.

The reporters laughed. "Come on, Bruce."

"Well," he said, and shrugged, "I've never thought much about it. I ski like I breathe, or talk, or . . ." He glanced to the side and smiled. "Or like I make love."

The girl he looked at was wearing a long silver nylon coat with a matching suit and turban. She appeared to be four or five years older than Scott, but she was attractive, and she smiled back as if anxious to please him.

"Who's the fashion plate?" Caroline asked.

"You don't know Tina Elliot—Mark Elliot's wife? She's the one who put him on top. And I mean that in more ways than one, dear."

The two ice skaters were getting the attention now. The one they were calling Annette was a little older and seemed more sure of herself. She was wearing a cloak over her skating costume, and she moved up close to Bruce Scott as she answered questions.

"Color Tina Elliot jealous," Mrs. Shelby said quietly.

Tina Elliot was watching closely, her face rigid as Bruce put his arm around the ice skater. The photographers snapped pictures and then the girl motioned to the other skater.

"Hey, Cathy! Come and get in the act!"

Caroline remembered the girl now. Her name was Cathy Jordan, and she was from somewhere on the Coast. She was rather petite compared to the other girl, and it looked as if she asked for her coach's approval before she stepped forward.

"You two girls will be competing with each other tomorrow, right?" a reporter asked.

9

"Well," Annette answered with a chuckle, "I must admit I've got my eye on the Shelby Cup. But so has Cathy."

Cathy Jordan tried to smile, but mostly she looked embarrassed. Bruce Scott squeezed her shoulder and then the trio broke up. Tina Elliot quickly moved to his side and smiled coolly as they walked away.

"I think there's going to be a lot more competition in the beds around here than there'll be on the slopes and ice rinks," Mrs. Shelby said.

Caroline smiled and moved toward the door. "I think I'll get settled in my room, Florence."

"Aren't you going to say hello to your ever-loving ex-husband?"

Caroline glanced back and saw David striding toward them from the other end of the terrace.

He looked as handsome as ever—maybe even more so. He was always as meticulous about his dress as he was about the details in a business contract, and now he was tanned and healthy-looking, and seemed to have an extra bounce in his step. When he spotted her his face brightened.

"Caroline! God, what a great way to start a day! It's terrific to see you . . . the two of you together. How are you?"

He gave his mother a quick kiss on the cheek. " 'Morning, sweetheart. Mom, what are you hanging around for? You and McDade have a full schedule. I want you to see everything that's going on around here."

"David, David, I will see it," she answered

10

wearily, "but let's sit a while and have a drink together."

"But, Mother, it's still morning."

"Yeah—late morning."

Shelby gave her a warm smile. "Mother, I really would like to spend some time with Caroline if you don't mind. Okay?"

Mrs. Shelby knew she was beaten. She grabbed McDade's arm as if he were a child, and walked him away. "Come on, McDade!"

Caroline watched them go, then felt David's steady gaze. "How was the trip?" he asked.

"Fine." She gave the hotel and the surroundings an admiring glance. "Quite a place."

"Thank you. Caroline, I ..."

One of the photographers suddenly moved to his side. "Mr. Shelby, any chance of getting a picture of the Shelby Cup?"

Caroline smiled, knowing what the answer would be. The building would have to be on fire before David Shelby would pass up a chance for more publicity. Particularly when the object to be photographed had his name on it.

"Sure," he answered. "Get some of the fellas together and come on over to my office. You know where it is, don't you?"

"We'll find it," the man said. He walked off, and Shelby lightly took Caroline's arm. "Come on. I want to show you something."

Caroline wanted to say no, but she knew it was hopeless. He guided her back into the lobby and began a grand tour of the place. This came from Mexico and that came from France, all at very high cost and much difficulty. The paintings were specially commissioned and the fountains were designed by the same man who had done them for Onassis.

They finally reached a small office, where an attractive girl was filing her nails behind the desk. Caroline wasn't surprised; David always had attractive secretaries, and their duties always seemed to be something other than typing or taking dictation. Oddly enough, it did not irritate her now.

"Susan Maxwell, this is Mrs. Shelby," he said. "Susan's my secretary. Did you reach Marty Brenner?" he asked the girl.

"Not yet."

"Try it again," he said, and ushered Caroline toward his office door.

"I just did," the girl said.

"Then try it once more," Shelby said more emphatically, and closed the door.

The room looked more like a library in a mansion than it did an office. The carpeting was plush and two of the walls were beautifully paneled—a baby-grand piano in the corner between them. The other two walls were solid glass and overlooked a frozen lake where a few people were ice-skating.

Caroline smiled as she watched him move from one window to the other. He was obviously pleased with his own creation.

"This is gorgeous," she said.

"Expensive!"

Caroline laughed. "David, you're something else!"

He moved to his desk, but then turned back, his eyes narrowed. "You checked in as Caroline Brace. Was that a put-down?"

"No. Just the way I feel."

"I changed it back to Caroline Shelby."

"No, David," she said with smile, "you'll never do that."

He gazed thoughtfully at her for a minute, then moved back to the window.

"You have done wonders," she said. She meant it sincerely, but she also wanted to change the subject.

"Yes, I have," he answered with some pride. "And it was a fight, baby. They said I'd destroy the environment."

"Yes, I read about it." She didn't understand all the technical aspects of his battle with the environmentalists, but when she read the stories she had little doubt about who would emerge victorious.

"I set out to open up this magnificent country to as many people as I could. And, by God, Caroline, I've done it. And it's going to keep growing. That's what I see, and that's what I'll do."

Caroline moved closer to the window, and he suddenly glanced at her and pointed down. "Does that look destructive? I'm creating a beautiful life here, Caroline. It's a great thing that's happening."

There was a determined note in his voice, as if he were a crusader battling an army of infidels. "Then what's wrong?" she asked quietly.

He looked sharply at her, then laughed. "You still see through me, don't you?"

"Yup," she answered. "You want to tell me about it?"

"All right," he said after a minute. "Senator Maybrook, who used to be one of the planning commissioners I had dealings with, is under investigation."

"For this?"

"Oh, no," he said quickly. "For some corporate connections."

"David, say it," she urged impatiently.

He hesitated again, then glanced off at his buzzing telephone. "I bought some of this land from one of those corporations."

"Isn't that a matter of public record?"

"Yes, and so is a sizable contribution I made to his subsequent senatorial campaign." He put the phone to his ear. "Yeah?" He listened a minute, then slammed the receiver down. "Dammit!"

"David, what are you going to do?"

He looked at her as if his thoughts were a million miles off, then burst out, "I'm gonna take you to lunch. I don't want to talk about this goddamn mess. You're here. I love that you're here. I love you. And how is your life? Are you still working for *Harper's Bazaar?*"

"Vogue," she said.

"I mean *Vogue.*" He grabbed the buzzing phone again. "Yeah! Who? Dammit! Send them in." He smiled apologetically as he put the receiver down. "Baby, I've gotta answer just a few questions for these press guys. Okay?"

"Be my guest," Caroline answered. She moved off toward the windows as the reporters and photographers came through the door.

David greeted them all as if they were long lost brothers, only stumbling over a couple of names. By his behavior he didn't have a trouble in the world.

"Well, what can I tell you gentlemen?" he finally asked. "You're about to see the greatest show on earth, courtesy of Shelby Enterprises."

"Can we see the cup?"

"With pleasure." He beamed and crossed the room. The cup was in a glass cabinet; a beautifully sculpted trophy that looked as if it weighed fifty pounds.

"Here it is, gentlemen." He held it high enough so all the photographers could get a clear picture.

"When you brought Gentileschi to the United States, did he come just for the design of the cup?" one of them asked.

"Well, mostly. But we were able to enjoy our time together, too. He's a terrific guy."

"Can we get a shot of you against the mountain?"

"Of course." Shelby crossed to the window, and Caroline edged away, moving unobtrusively toward the door.

"Mr. Shelby," a hard-voiced reporter asked, "how much help was Senator Maybrook in getting you the variance for this development? Especially when so many before you had failed?"

It was a loaded question and Caroline looked back to see how Shelby would field it. But he was wearing a boy-scout face and didn't hesitate.

"The senator shared my philosophy about this development, and his efforts were considerable. Senator Maybrook is a fine man and I respect him very much. I'm sure the public shares my opinion."

Another reporter asked, "Was the design concept for the Shelby Cup your idea or Mr. Gentileschi's?"

The man who was interested in the senator didn't give him a chance to answer. "Mr. Shelby," he said icily, "you were pretty brave to gamble the extraordinary option money you did before you got clearance. Would you care to tell us if you had some assurance from government agencies that the project would be okayed?"

Caroline opened the door and was almost out when he called to her. "Sweetheart," he said, instead of answering the reporter's question, "a half hour, forty-five minutes at the most. Lunch, right? Promise?"

Caroline smiled and closed the door behind her.

"Well, Tonino and I worked on the cup design together," she could hear Shelby saying. "He's a very open person that way. What we did was ..."

The girl at the desk was filing her nails again. She glanced curiously at Caroline. "Can I help you with something?"

Caroline moved toward the outer door. "No, but I think your boss could use some help."

The girl's eyes widened. "What's the matter?"

"One of those reporters in there is trying to nail him to a cross."

Caroline didn't look back to see the girl's reaction. She moved down the hall, trying to recall the number of her room and wondering where it might be. Then she remembered the key in her purse. Number 204.

It was a comfortable-looking room—a suite, really, with a couch and chairs and television in the sitting room and then a king-size bed in the bedroom. And her suitcases were there.

She smiled as she stretched out on the bed, wondering if David had had something in mind when he assigned her king-size accommodations. Probably. And maybe, as in some old European castles, there was a secret passage coming directly from his room into her fireplace.

She was tired. She had risen before dawn to catch the six-o'clock flight, and she was not accustomed to farmers' hours. And she had lost two more hours coming west. My God, she realized, it was almost three o'clock in New York. And she still hadn't eaten lunch.

2

◇◇◇◇◇◇◇◇◇◇◇◇◇◇◇◇◇◇◇◇◇◇◇◇◇◇◇◇◇◇◇

Florence Shelby did not like cold weather, and she liked snow even less. In La Jolla, California, right now the temperature was probably a balmy sixty-eight, and all her friends would be on the terrace of Mabel Stringer's house sipping martinis and watching the sailboats go by.

But Florence's fate was to have a hyperactive son who thought he was a genius, and needed his mother to pat him on the head and tell him he was doing a fine job. So she had brought all her fur coats and purchased some long underwear, and she was doing her duty.

She would much rather have operated from the cocktail lounge, sipping Bloody Marys. But David had insisted that she have a guided tour of every square foot of his creation, and the poor little bookkeeper, McDade, wouldn't dare deviate from the itinerary outlined by the great man.

"Those are all condominiums over there," he said as the hotel car thumped along on its snow chains. "When the project is finished, there will be two hundred and forty of them, at an average cost of seventy-seven thousand dollars. They're an extremely good investment if you're in a tax position where you—"

"Never mind, McDade. Let's just get it over with as fast as we can, huh? What are those crazy people doing?"

"Those are snowmobiles, Mrs. Shelby."

To Florence they looked more like the bump-'em cars they used to have in amusement parks. And the people racing around in them looked like a bunch of drunks. "You'll never get me in one of those," she said.

"And that's the ski lift over there. When we're finished there'll be seven of them, providing the greatest elevation drop in the entire western hemisphere."

"Then you'll never get me on one of those, either."

"Not even by moonlight?"

Florence glanced sharply at the little man, wondering if she had heard what she thought she had heard. She guessed she had, because McDade's face reddened as he turned away.

"Why, you devil, you," she said with a smile.

They were coming into the village now, and McDade slowed the car down to a creep. "This is called SkiHaven," he said. "There are forty-three shops and four restaurants. There's also a fire department and a—"

"Candy-ass," Florence said.

"I beg your pardon?"

"Candy-ass," she repeated. "Haven't you ever seen a candy-ass town before? It's like Carmel, California, or Solvang. Or Disneyland. Everything is quaint and cute, and the stores charge twice the prices for the same junk you can buy at K-Mart or J. C. Penney's."

McDade was blushing again.

"Looks like David ordered everything except the people," Florence remarked. The stores all seemed to be in business and waiting, but there wasn't a customer in sight.

"Oh, they've been ordered," McDade said. "We've got buses coming in tomorrow. And a package tour arriving at the hotel tonight. Two to a room, complimentary breakfast, and a bottle of champagne."

"Well, well," Florence said.

She finally saw what looked like a customer. A man in a uniform was coming out of a drugstore carrying a package. He waved at Mc-Dade.

"Who's that?" Florence asked.

"Phil Prentiss, the snow ranger. He patrols the snow and checks it."

"What's to check? It's all white and cold, isn't it?"

"Well, your snow is a variable element, Mrs. Shelby. It turns hard or soft, wet or dry, according to the weather. You've got to keep checking it to see what it's up to."

"Huh. That's the way David feels about me. Maybe he should hire a handsome snow ranger to look me over now and then. I think I'll suggest it to him."

They were out of the village now and passing clusters of newly built chalets. "SkiHaven Estates," McDade said with a sweep of his hand. "Our chalet-development project for winter-sports lovers." He gave her an eager smile. "You'll notice all but one of them has been sold."

Florence nodded and yawned. "Congratulations." The high altitude was getting to her, she decided.

"Just one more thing to look at, Mrs. Shelby. I think you'll find this interesting."

"Why?"

"It's Mr. Shelby's personal chalet."

Florence nodded, and McDade drove on through a wooded area to a broad slope overlooking the entire valley. There was nothing more than the foundation of the house so far, and a number of workmen were felling huge trees on the adjacent slopes.

McDade helped her out of the car and took a firm grip on her arm as they moved up the snowbank. "I expect Mr. Shelby showed you the plans?"

"David hasn't shown me a thing."

"It's going to be three stories, with the master bedroom on top. Also a solarium, an indoor pool, and a genuine Finnish sauna. In fact, Mr. Shelby is having it shipped over from Finland."

"Why doesn't he just build the place in Finland?"

"I beg your pardon?"

"Nothing," Florence said.

A screeching saw bit into a tree, and Florence covered her ears. McDade gestured across the slope and shouted close to her, "Mr. Shelby wants to create an uninterrupted view! That's why they're clearing out that area."

"It seems stupid to cut down such pretty trees," Florence yelled back. She winced as the power saw suddenly went silent and the tree slowly began to fall, then crashed into the snow.

On the road below, Nick Thorne had just eased his Jeep around the hotel car and parked in front of it. Then he watched grimly as the hundred-foot pine thudded into the snow and sent twigs and branches flying. One more down, he thought to himself as he pushed the door open. At the rate Shelby was going, the area would soon be the coldest desert on earth.

He didn't bother taking his cameras out of the jeep. He already had a thousand pictures of denuded forests, and he had no interest in documenting the rape of another one.

Thorne was thirty-two years old and a professional photographer by occupation. But sometimes he wondered if there would be anything left in the world worth taking pictures of.

"Hi, Mr. Thorne," the construction foreman said. He was holding a set of blueprints and looking over the foundation of Shelby's chalet.

"How're you doing, Pauley?"

The man frowned and rolled up the blueprints. "Say, you were right about that salt lick. It's gettin' kinda low. Them elk been comin' down from Big Face ever since the high winds."

Thorne had noticed the number of elk

moving down from the higher elevations and he had distributed salt blocks for them around the valley. "I'll bring some more tomorrow," he said.

The man who had just cut down the tree was moving toward them, his power saw dangling from his hand. He was wearing a hard-hat, and the stub of a cold cigar was wedged into the side of his mouth. He nodded at Thorne. "Whatdya say?"

"Your boss tell you guys to cut those trees that close to the ground?"

"Right down to the roots if we can."

"Mr. Shelby and the architect decided it was desirable," McDade said behind Thorne. "Your smooth slope and your clean lines."

Thorne looked at the little man and the bundled-up woman standing beside him.

"Mr. Thorne," McDade said, "this is Mrs. Shelby. Mr. Shelby's mother."

Thorne nodded. The woman didn't look like the kind who would have given birth to a monster like Shelby. But you never knew.

Thorne moved up the slope to where a snow shovel was sticking out of a drift. He scooped a pile of packed snow into it and tossed the chunk across the slope to a point just below the newly cut tree stump. The snow landed with a *thunk*, but it didn't tumble any farther.

Pauley smiled. "It's apt to stick, Mr. Thorne."

Thorne nodded and tossed the shovel back into the drift. The snow was sticky enough to hold, but that wouldn't necessarily be true when the temperature changed, or if another foot or two fell during the night.

"Nice to meet you, ma'am," he said to Mrs. Shelby, and headed down the slope. When he reached the jeep he paused and looked back.

The workman had started his power saw again, chewing it into another tree. Thorne watched, his eyes fixed on the glob of snow as the screech of the saw grew more strident. The snow seemed to quiver for a minute. Then, as if it wore a clump of dry gravel, it disintegrated and scattered down the slope.

"What's the gimmick?" Florence called down from above.

"It was the saw," Thorne answered. "Sound can move snow, and that slope is not stable. With the trees gone, it's dangerous."

"You mean all of this snow could slide down the hill?" she asked.

"That's right, Mrs. Shelby. And all that snow on the slope two thousand feet above you." Thorne gave her a grim smile, then climbed in his jeep and drove off.

"Who is he?" Florence asked McDade.

"He's a photographer who lives up here. Sort of a loner. All the time in the world for nature. No time for people."

"It's a point of view."

"Well, there's certainly nothing to worry about, Mrs. Shelby. Your son has had the best engineers in the country check out the land and structures. And of course the government okayed the environmental-impact reports."

"And the man coming out of the drugstore checks the snow, right?"

"That's right."

'At the ice rink, Cathy Jordan glided smoothly through a broad counterclockwise circle, her arms spread and relaxed, her left leg outstretched, toe pointing. When the circle was almost complete she swung the left leg down, easing the skate smoothly onto the ice. At the same time, her right leg rose gracefully behind her and she was now making a clockwise circle, completing her figure eight.

When the circle was closed, she moved toward the edge of the rink, gathering speed, keeping her head high. She smiled as she passed Leo, her coach. Then she circled back into the center of the ring, turning another circle with her skates heel-to-heel. Then she suddenly felt tense as she glimpsed Annette and her coach leaning against the rail watching her.

It was ridiculous that Annette's presence should bother her, and Leo had told her a hundred times to forget it and concentrate only on what she was doing. But for some reason that made it worse. She was not only conscious of Annette smiling at her, but she was now conscious of Leo growling and growing angry.

She reversed the circle and gently swung her arms in preparation for her spin. But then, for no more than half an instant, she suddenly came to a dead stop before she swung up on her toe and began the spin.

At the rail Annette smiled. "She's a little off center. Just like in Toronto last year."

Craig Harmon, her coach, nodded and quietly lit a cigar. "That may be lucky for you."

Annette gave him a sour glance and

watched as Cathy spun faster, almost into a blur. "Maybe she wasn't off center after all." The girl was good, there was no question about that. If she ever got over her nervousness, she could be great. "Atta girl, Cathy!" she called out, and clapped her hands.

As if the words of encouragement had struck her like a snowball, Cathy's spin no longer had its smooth precision. She was like a top losing momentum. She quickly let herself slow down, fighting for balance.

"It's all right, baby, it's okay," Leo said. He pushed away from the railing and skated to her side. "Just take it easy."

Cathy came to an abrupt halt, and Leo reached out to stop her from falling.

She looked like she was close to tears. "No, it's not all right, Leo. I always do it."

Leo pulled her around to block her view of Annette and her coach. "Don't beat yourself, baby. You are beautiful; you're doing beautifully."

"But when I saw her . . ."

"You let it get to you. You forget how beautiful you are. Don't forget that, baby. Love yourself. When you start that spin, you find your spot and you go. Spot and go. Spot and go. And you don't let anything in the world knock you off balance."

Leo guided her toward the opposite end of the rink, continuing to soothe her.

"Why don't you ever do that for me?" Annette said to Harmon as she buckled on her skates.

"You get enough romance on your own, kid."

Annette gave him a quick glance and smiled. "I have no idea what you're talking about."

"That Bruce Scott character, for one. I'd lay off him if I were you. Mrs. Tina Elliot's got her name written all over him in indelible ink, and it looks to me like she's got sharp claws."

"I'm not so sure Bruce likes sharp claws. In fact, I rather think he might like something soft and warm—and perhaps someone a little more energetic than Mrs. Elliot."

She gave him a haughty smile and moved out on the ice, gliding effortlessly into a routine very much like the one Cathy had just finished. She made the circles, head high, smiling, obviously enjoying herself, at the same time demonstrating an unshakable confidence.

She did a quick spin, then gathered speed and did a triple jump. From that she made a daringly sharp turn and went into a spin that was as fast as Cathy's had been. Then in a cool display of one-upmanship she dropped into a sit-spin, rose unerringly into an upright position, and then finished off with a graceful pirouette. She followed this with a broad sweep around the rink, made several jumps and loops, and ended up with a spray of ice as she came to a showy stop.

Harmon watched it all thoughtfully, noting the little things—the slight heaviness in her arms and the lack of height in her jumps. Annette would never be a world-class champion. She didn't have that inspired flair and the dedication that would lift her above all the other competitors. It was something Cathy Jordan had, and would make her a superstar in a year or two.

But what the hell, he thought. He was earning four hundred and fifty a week plus expenses to stroke Annette's ego, and she was probably still good for two or three more years.

"Great," he said when she finished.

On the south side of the ridge the snow was soft and moist, which made the going a little too rough for Bruce Scott. He dug his poles in and worked his way back to the top, then schussed along through the sparse growth of trees. The wind was picking up a little, and swirling gusts of snow swept off the ridge and sent stinging particles into his face.

He finally stopped and leaned heavily on one of his poles, admiring the scenery. Far below and to the left, the hotel and SkiHaven Village looked like tiny dollhouses nestling in a bed of whipped cream. To the right the canyon dropped, and he could make out the little bridge and the ribbon of paved road disappearing down the side of the mountain.

The slope directly in front of him looked good. There were a few trees scattered along the left side, and on the right a treacherous-looking escarpment formed a solid wall that ran almost to the bottom. But between the trees and the escarpment the natural trough formed a perfect ski run. Scott pulled his goggles down and moved closer to the edge. He checked over his bindings, tightened his gloves, and then pushed off.

He angled from side to side, doing a few light jump turns first, getting the feel of the snow. It was a little heavier than he liked, and there was some shifting, but it didn't seem to cause any problems. He let himself gather more speed and took a long angle toward the trees on the left.

This was the part of skiing he loved—to be alone and racing down virgin slopes.

When he reached the trees he had intended to angle back. Instead, he suddenly grinned and let himself fly past the first of the heavily laden pines. Then he whipped through a sharp turn and headed straight down the slope. The challenge was more dangerous now. He was plummeting down at full speed, the trees whirling past him as he shifted left and right, feeling the tips of the branches flick at his arms and legs.

There was no sound, and he felt only a faint vibration in the earth at first. Then he heard it—a steadily growing rumble from somewhere on the slope behind him. He dug the edges of his skis in a little harder, risking a quick backward glance. Then he took a split second more as he gaped at the torrent of snow and the tumbling slabs of ice. It was an avalanche! The thrashing wall of snow and flying ice was less than a hundred yards behind him, and he knew its speed was probably twice his own.

He felt his heart pounding into his throat as he crouched low and angled himself straight down the slope. Could he cut off to the side and get out of it? No, he quickly decided. To the right was the wall, and to the left the snow rose higher, forming the other edge of the trough.

He found himself counting the seconds as the ground shuddered and the roar behind him became almost deafening. Five, four, three, two . . . Then he swung himself sharply to the left, driving the edges of his skis deep into the soft snow as he headed for a tree.

He struck the trunk hard with his left arm, almost tearing it from the socket as he swung around the tree and came to an abrupt stop on the lower side of it. At the same instant, heavy snow and chunks of ice roared past him in an angry, tumbling swirl.

Three seconds later it was over. A few random pieces tumbled down or slid a few feet farther, and then there was suddenly silence.

Scott rested his head against the tree for a minute and caught his breath. Then he sighed heavily and smiled. He released his bindings and took a couple minutes to dig his skis from under the loose snow. Then he snapped them back on his boots and pushed off again, angling gently down the last two hundred yards of tumbled terrain.

He hadn't realized there was a cabin at the bottom of the slope, or that he had an audience. A man in Levi's and a plaid shirt was leaning against a shovel, gazing thoughtfully at him. He was only about thirty, but he had the craggy look of an old mountaineer or a fur trapper.

"You were damn lucky," the man said. "And smart."

Scott slid to a stop and looked back at the slopes. "You mean grabbing the tree? That's an old trick."

"It's a good trick if there happens to be a tree to grab. And if the avalanche doesn't happen to be big enough to knock down the tree."

"Yeah, you got a point there."

"What are you doing out here? You're skiing the Big Face tomorrow, aren't you?"

Scott smiled. The trembling in his hands was finally easing off a little. "Just felt like practicing on my own. Away from the crowd."

"You ought to check conditions first."

Scott laughed. "I just did."

"You want a lift back to the hotel?"

"I'd appreciate that, pal."

"The name's Nick Thorne."

Scott shook the leathery hand. "Bruce Scott." He knelt to take his skis off. "Aren't you the guy who tried to stop Shelby from building all this?"

"I'm one of them."

"You don't like to see people enjoy the great outdoors, huh?"

"Not if they end up ruining every goddamn mountain and forest in the country doing it."

Scott slid his skis into the holders on the roof of the jeep. "Man, this whole world is likely to be blown up before you and I reach old age. There'll be plenty of pristine mountains and forests left after that."

Thorne smiled and banged the door shut. "It'll be blown up if people like Shelby have their way. In the meantime, I'd rather take my chances on things working out a little better."

Scott laughed. "Man, I'm going to take it while I can get it."

3

◇◇◇◇◇◇◇◇◇◇◇◇◇◇◇◇◇◇◇◇◇◇◇◇◇◇◇◇◇◇

Caroline blinked at the unfamiliar ceiling, then looked at the clock on the dresser. Two-fifteen. She must have gone to sleep the minute she lay down.

She smiled wryly to herself as she went into the bathroom and rinsed her face. David hadn't called. He was probably still talking to the reporters, trying to evade questions about Commissioner Maybrook.

She changed into a sweater and a pair of more comfortable pants. Then she gave herself a good hard look in the mirror.

What in the world was she doing here? In New York there were plenty of men who were interested in her; men who led normal, sane lives and seemed to have no desire to run hers. Was she still in love with David? Or was it just some kind of fascination—like watching somebody juggle ten plates at once? Seeing him in action again had brought back a lot of old memories.

She had no doubt that when she had married him she had been in love with him. But that was five years ago, and at the time he shared everything with her. There was even time to visit art galleries and go to Broadway plays, and they even took off for Europe for a month one spring. But the richer he got and the more big deals he made, the less she saw of him. Her role suddenly became that of an on-call hostess and part-time secretary. Three important men were coming in from Tokyo—could she arrange for cocktails at the apartment? "I have to be in Berlin on Tuesday and Rome on Thursday, and then back in New York by Saturday morning, so there's no point in your coming along. Why don't you go out to La Jolla and visit Florence? I know she'd be glad to see you."

For a long while there was the belief that it would come to an end. He would make the final big deal, and then he would sit back and rest on his laurels and his millions. It had taken Caroline two years to realize that no such thing would ever happen. It was like expecting a heroin addict to be happy and quit mainlining once he got a big dose of the best heroin on the market.

When she told him she was leaving him, he seemed shocked. But his response was typical. You can't, he said. It was the most ridiculous thing he had ever heard, and he couldn't understand why a woman who had everything in the world wanted to give it up. Then he sweetened the deal by giving her a new Mercedes and a trip to Hawaii with Florence. How could anyone turn down a deal like that? It worked when he was putting together mergers or trying to swing a real-estate deal. Why didn't it work on Caroline?

She almost felt sorry for him at times. In many ways he was like a little boy; he couldn't understand why everybody in the world wasn't happy when handed a piece of candy.

Had he grown up in the past two years? That, she supposed, was why she had come to Colorado—to see if he was still addicted to candy.

She smiled as she walked back to his office. She had waited for lunch so long she wasn't hungry anymore. She turned the last corner and strode through the door of his secretary's office.

Gary Buckner, the great ski jumper, was sitting on the girl's desk, leaning toward her with one hand under her chin.

"But it isn't breaking training," he was saying. "It's relaxing."

There wasn't much doubt about what was going on, and the girl's face suddenly went red to confirm it. "He's on the phone, Mrs. Shelby," she said to Caroline, and quickly pulled away from Buckner. "He finally got through to his lawyer."

Caroline gave both of them a sweet smile. "Thank you," she said, and went into the inner office.

David's face was also red, but it wasn't from embarrassment. He was pacing behind his desk, holding the phone to his ear.

"Goddammit, Marty, don't argue with

me," he snarled. "Get your ass up here!"

He motioned for Caroline to sit down, but she moved quietly to the windows.

"Well, something is going on, dammit! This morning some snot-nosed reporter started asking me about Maybrook and the land! . . . How do I know what he's after? But I don't like it, Marty. Yeah . . . it could mean a lot, and your ass could be in a sling too."

He listened for a minute, and his voice suddenly turned cold. "I want *you* and that whole goddamned file on the plane and up here by tomorrow night! You understand? . . . Okay!" He slammed the receiver down.

For another minute Caroline gazed at the top of the mountains, watching the wind sweep misty snow off the crests. Then she turned back. David's face was still red, and he was breathing heavily, as if unable to control his anger.

"Just give me a minute," he said. "Just a minute." He took a sip of water and rubbed his forehead. "God, it's hard to come down from that guy." He glanced at Caroline and frowned. "Don't give me that I-don't-approve look."

"I don't approve or disapprove of anything you do. You're like Niagara Falls. You just happen. What is it you're afraid of?"

"I'm not afraid of anything. Everything I've done has been perfectly legal. It's just that those . . . those newspaper bastards want to make it look like some kind of under-the-table deal. As if I bought off the senator."

"Did you?"

"I gave him a campaign contribution. And it just so happens that he was in favor of developing this property too. Is that so bad? What the hell. I gave his opponent a contribution too."

Caroline shrugged. "I guess the senator has a right to an opinion the same as anybody else. By the way, I came to collect lunch."

He looked surprised.

"You know," Caroline said, "where you sit down at a table and a waiter brings you food."

"Oh, God, lunch! Right." He moved to the window and took her in his arms. The kiss was lingering and passionate.

"Supremacy tactics," Caroline said when he let her go.

"Once in a while they work. Come on."

In the outer office Susan was thumbing through a magazine. "Be back in an hour," David told her. He put an arm around Caroline as they moved down the hall. "You're good for me, Caroline. It's great to have you back again."

"You don't have me back again."

"Well, you know what I mean."

"How am I good for you?"

"You're levelheaded, and keep things in perspective. Sometimes I get a little caught up in the idea that everything has to be perfect. I guess everybody can't be one hundred percent on my side."

"Fifty-one percent is all you need to get elected president."

David laughed, but he was also glancing

around, making sure everything was going exactly right as they moved across the lobby toward the stairs.

"Shelby!" a harsh voice called out from behind them.

The man coming across the lobby looked like a lumberjack. But there was a cold intelligence in the hard blue eyes. Shelby smiled, but he seemed to brace himself as they paused.

"Nick! Glad to see you. I want you to meet somebody."

"Shelby, we've got to talk," the man said. "You're crazy to be cutting those trees over by that house you're building."

Shelby ignored the statement. "Caroline, I want you to meet Nick Thorne. I'm sure you're familiar with his work."

Caroline knew the work of Nick Thorne very well, but until now she'd had little hope of ever meeting him face to face. Nick Thorne was almost a legendary name in the field of photography. But most of his pictures were from the North Pole, or deepest Africa, or the jungles of Central America. Somehow he seemed out of place in a fancy Colorado hotel. "Of course I know his work," she said.

"Nick, this is my wife, Caroline."

Nick Thorne didn't seem to have the slightest interest. "Hello, Mrs. Shelby," he said with a glance. "I'm telling you, David, without that cover, everything below that place you're building, all the way down to the lake, is open to slides."

David grasped Caroline's arm and moved up the stairs. "Nick, I'll be back later this afternoon. We'll talk, okay?"

"You said that last week. I want to talk now."

Shelby stopped and glanced at his watch. To Caroline's surprise he gave her an apologetic smile. "Sweetheart, I'm sorry, I want to talk to Nick. Twenty minutes . . . a half an hour at the most . . . then, lunch. Promise!"

Caroline returned the smile and moved up the stairs. "I'll see you at dinner, David."

"Sweetheart, dinner's the banquet. We won't have any time."

"No, but I know you'll *be* there. Nice to have met you, Mr. Thorne."

"Caroline!"

"We'll wave at each other," she said, and continued up the stairs.

Shelby watched her disappear around the corner, then moved down the stairs. "Let's go in the bar, Nick."

Aside from the barman, the only person in the place was Tina Elliot. She was in a far corner with a magazine and a brandy snifter, now wearing huge tinted glasses and a T-shirt with the name BRUCE stenciled across the front. Shelby waved to her and leaned heavily against the bar.

"Goddammit, Nick, you're a hard man to talk to. Now, simmer down. There just isn't enough hazard above that slope to carry on about."

"There is hazard, Shelby. These mountains have gotten along without you very well since the beginning of time. You march in here with your big dreams of enterprise and want to rearrange the whole thing."

"No, Nick, share it." He turned to the

waiting bartender. "Scotch on the rocks, Harry. How about you, Nick?"

"Nothing." Nick waited until the bartender moved off. "You're risking the lives of everyone you're inviting up here to share it with."

"Now, Nick, just hold on. That routine may have worked in front of the commission, but now you're dealing with me. I want people to enjoy this land. I don't want to bury them in it."

"Well, they're sure as hell going to be buried if . . ." Thorne glanced toward the door as Phil Prentiss came in.

"Phil," Shelby said, "come on over here."

Phil Prentiss was an easygoing man who tried to keep everybody happy. Thorne didn't expect any help from him.

"Hi, Nick, David," Prentiss said. "Glad I caught you. I want to get those figures and rosters on your ski patrol tomorrow, David. You're going to have a lot of people up on those slopes."

"Phil," Shelby said, "will you, as a professional, tell this lunatic about today's reports?"

"What reports?"

"The snow—the whole goddamned thing."

Prentiss looked at Thorne and smiled. "Again, Nick? Come on. The whole place is stable. Every survey is on the nose."

Nick sighed. "Phil, I don't want to hear about the surveys. I know what they say. At least you can dynamite Old Frown, she has always been the most dangerous peak around here."

"I've fired every cornice that has ever caused a slide problem. Old Frown was fired just twenty-seven days ago."

"But Old Frown's building again, Phil. We've had a hell of a lot of snow since twenty-seven days ago. And with the storm heading in tonight, and all those people climbing the slopes, you can't ignore the hazard."

"I'm not ignoring anything. We're okay for all normal circumstances."

"This isn't normal, Phil, and you know it. There's a heaviness around here, and it's growing. The whole place is getting heavier. I can feel it."

Shelby downed his drink and slammed it on the bar. "Goddammit, I've had it. You want the whole population to panic because you feel heaviness? I'll tell you something, Thorne. I'm not moving on your presentiments and premonitions. I move on my own judgment. You know what'll happen if Phil goes up there and starts triggering off snow slides? Assuming the snow is even heavy enough to start any slides, every damned slope in this valley would be piled with boulders and ice slabs. So how in the hell is anybody going to ski on that? And I've got the country's two best skiers up here, and a whole television crew coming in to film them. I'm not going to blow that, Thorne. Not just because you have a feeling of heaviness." He pushed his empty glass away and grabbed Prentiss' arm. "Come on, Phil, I'll get you those damned papers."

Nick watched them go—David Shelby already talking to Prentiss about something else.

"You really think that stuff is getting

ready to come down, Mr. Thorne?" the bartender asked.

Thorne looked at him, a little surprised. It was the first time anybody had shown any real interest in his opinions. "I think there's a good chance of it, Harry."

"But how about those rangers? Don't they check those things pretty close? I mean, it's their job, isn't it?"

"Not necessarily. And the government has never been famous for moving fast. Maybe next week, or next month, or next winter they'll get around to giving the place a thorough check. Maybe by then somebody will look at a piece of paper and see how many thousands of trees Shelby has cut down to make his beautiful Olympic ski runs."

"Yeah, I suppose you're right."

"And have you ever heard of a meteorologist who could predict exactly how much snow is going to fall during a storm?"

The man smiled. "Can't say as I have. And it looks like we've got one coming, don't it?"

Caroline changed into a bathing suit and took the elevator down to the combination indoor-outdoor pool she had noticed earlier. As long as she was not eating, she might as well go the whole distance and do something for her figure too.

She had the whole place to herself. The inside was done in a Western motif—barstools covered with unborn-calf skin, Remington winter paintings on the walls. She tested the water with a toe and plunged in.

She had forgotten how much she had enjoyed swimming. She glided downward almost to the bottom and swam under the glass to the outside area. When she surfaced she found herself looking up at Nick Thorne. He was standing with his hands in his rear pockets, squinting off at the mountains.

"Hi, there!" she said.

He looked startled, as though she were some deep-sea creature emerging from the depths. "Oh . . . Mrs. Shelby."

"Brace is the name now. We're divorced."

He smiled as if pleased by the news. "Yeah. Well, I knew I'd seen you somewhere before."

"Yes. About fifteen minutes ago. In the lobby."

"No, before that."

Caroline laughed. "Probably on David's desk. In a frame."

"Yeah . . . that must be it. Your ex-husband is a tough guy."

"Tough . . . or stubborn?" Caroline asked. She breast-stroked her way along the side of the pool.

"Maybe a little of both. You like him?"

She stopped and held onto the gutter. "Let me think about that. I don't know. I might even love him."

He nodded, thinking it over, then looked at the mountains again. Caroline followed his gaze.

"I hope there's going to be a snowstorm," she said. "While I'm here, I want to see the works. And there's a great thing about snowstorms. They make the world seem different."

"Different is better?"

Caroline shrugged. "Don't you think so?"

"No. Things look pretty good from here."

He was looking directly at her when he said it. Caroline smiled. He was the most attractive man she had seen so far in David's mountain paradise.

"It's pretty chilly," he remarked. "You must be cold in there."

"It's not too bad in the water." He was gazing thoughtfully at her as if wondering if she belonged to the jet-set and winter-sports crowd that was occupying most of the hotel. "Come on inside," Caroline said, and ducked into the water. She slid under the partition again and breast-stroked across the inner pool.

"You going to the big party tonight?" she asked, moving up the steps. "Or don't you like that kind of thing?"

"No. I'm afraid I don't feel like celebrating all this."

"You'd rather put a couple sticks of dynamite under it, huh?"

He smiled. "I wouldn't go quite that far."

"Well, I hope you change your mind and come."

Nick watched her dry her hair, her firm breasts beautifully contoured as she worked the towel over her scalp. "Where do you usually hang out?" he asked.

"In New York. I'm in the fashion business."

"I'm not surprised."

She laughed and picked up her robe. "Not that way. I'm an editor at *Vogue* magazine."

"That's better yet. You're a prospective customer for my pictures."

Caroline gave him a surprised look. "Mr. Thorne, I have on several occasions attempted to buy some of your pictures for fashion layouts. But your New York agent wants a small fortune just for a snapshot."

"Of course. How else do you think I pay for my African safaris?"

"Humph! How about selling me a couple pictures from the zoo instead?"

He smiled. "You sound like your ex-husband. Put all the animals in a zoo and turn the jungles into parking lots."

"Yes, I guess you're right. I forgot you're a purist." She had her robe tied and her sandals on. She gazed at him for a minute, wishing he would ask her to lunch. But he had probably been up since dawn and had eaten lunch promptly at twelve o'clock. "Well . . . it's been nice talking to you, Mr. Thorne."

He nodded and waited until she was at the door before he spoke. "By the way, the name is Nick."

She smiled back. "And mine's Caroline."

Thorne watched her go, then headed back through the lobby. She didn't appear to be the kind of woman Shelby would have picked for a wife. Or—more accurately, maybe—one that would have picked Shelby. She seemed too sensible for that.

After he pushed through the front door and was outside, he paused for a minute on the steps. A big Greyhound-type tour bus was parked in front with all kinds of people piling

47

out the door. Bellboys were getting suitcases
and skis from the luggage compartment while
the passengers were looking things over.

"Who needs Switzerland?" a heavyset
woman exclaimed, looking at the mountain
peaks.

Her husband was all bundled up in a
mackinaw and wool mittens. "That's what the
ad said." He beamed. "And by golly, I don't
think they did the place justice. Look at the
snow up there, honey."

"Jason!" a woman shouted with alarm.
Her cry came a half second too late; her nine-
or ten-year-old boy had just let a snowball fly,
and it caromed off the shoulder of the heavy
woman.

"Well, I never!" She scowled.

"Jason, stop it!" the boy's mother com-
manded. She was about thirty-five, dressed in
a fur-lined jacket and boots and hurrying over
from a big Mercedes. "I'm sorry," she said to
the couple. She grabbed the boy's arm and hus-
tled him off. "He's just overexcited."

"All kids seem to be overexcited these
days," the woman muttered to her husband.

"It's all this breast-feeding," the man said
as they brushed past Thorne.

Nick smiled and moved down the steps and
across the parking lot. When he reached his
jeep he paused for a minute, looking at Phil
Prentiss' Forest Service truck. After a glance
at the hotel, he moved around to the back of
the truck and looked at the jumble of equipment. There were ropes, portable lamps, avalanche probes, shovels, first-aid kits . . . He
opened a locker-type box and studied the con-

tents for a minute. He opened a second one and finally found what he was looking for. He dug out a handful of shells and quickly shoved them into his pocket.

4

<><><><><><><><><><><><><><><><><><><><><><><><>

Mark Elliot had put on his dark glasses as quickly as the plane landed in Cedar Falls. Sometimes they worked, and he could slip through an airport without being recognized. But while he was waiting for his bags, people were once again staring at him. He smiled and waited patiently, once more paying the price of being a celebrity.

When the hotel driver came, and they started climbing into the mountains, he removed the glasses and enjoyed the scenery.

He had mixed feelings about coming to Colorado. David Shelby was a friend, he supposed. But it was one of those "commercial" friendships that Elliot seemed to pick up by the thousands. Shelby always remembered him at Christmas and on his birthday, and he invited him to a couple dozen cocktail parties every year. Was it because of the Mark Elliot television show, and the fact that one of Shelby's enterprises might get a nationwide plug? Or was it because Shelby genuinely liked him?

It didn't make a whole lot of difference, Elliot decided. There were thousands of people in the world with whom he had the same kind of relationship. And if he looked at it from the other side, Shelby was also doing him a favor by gathering enough celebrities at his lodge that he could probably get a couple shows out of it. Bruce Scott and Gary Buckner would be good guests, and he could run a lot of footage of the two of them on the slopes. And the same would be true for the two ice skaters. Exclusive films of the competition for the Shelby Cup.

Elliot smiled at the idea. Shelby's promoting something like the Shelby Cup competition was pretentious as hell, and five years from now it would be nothing more than a footnote in the sports almanacs. But he was pouring enough money into its promotion that he would probably get his hotel off to a good start. Unless the skiers didn't happen to show up. Or one of them broke a leg before the competition started. Which wouldn't surprise Elliot too much. David Shelby was a thorough man, and that was probably his biggest flaw. He got so wrapped up in details, and had his fingers so deeply into every facet of his projects, that he often overlooked the obvious. Which was why he neglected his wife, and hadn't even known she was unhappy until the day she announced she was going to divorce him.

Elliot gazed out the car window at the towering peaks and sighed heavily. He was the last one to be critical of a man who had lost his wife in a divorce court. The same thing was going to happen to him very shortly, and it was going to be far more painful than it had been for Shelby. At least Caroline had not been sleeping with every suntanned young stud who came strutting down the pike.

To hell with it, he finally thought. It was good to get away from New York for a while, and he might as well enjoy the mountains.

The driver pulled up in front of the lodge and opened the car door for him. "This is it, sir. I'll get your bags."

Elliot stepped out and took a deep breath, admiring the building. At least Shelby's attention to details paid off in some ways. The place was beautiful.

Two bellboys grabbed the bags, and Elliot gave the driver a twenty-dollar bill.

"Oh, no, sir," the man protested. "It's all part of the hotel service."

Elliot stuck the bill in the man's coat pocket and moved up the steps. "It was a nice ride, I enjoyed it."

"Thank you, sir. Thank you very much."

The lobby was mobbed with people, all of them apparently trying to check in at once. Heads started turning and mouths came open as they gaped at him.

He smiled and moved past the crowd toward the bar. Then a familiar voice stopped him.

"Mark, Mark! How are you? It's good to see you!"

Shelby was coming across the lobby, his face beaming. "Hullo, David—it's good to be here."

"Hey, you're looking great. Really great,

53

Mark! Come on, we'll get you settled. Where are your bags?"

The two bellboys were still behind him. "I think these are mine."

"Good, good. Sammy, take Mr. Elliot's things to suite 509. Come on, Mark."

Elliot had the feeling he had run into a windmill every time he saw Shelby. He smiled and looked around the lobby. "Take it easy, David. Just let me catch a few breaths of this fantastic air first."

"It's great, isn't it?" Shelby glanced at the front door. "Uh . . . when does your crew arrive?"

"Noon tomorrow. Is Scott here?"

"Yeah, everybody's here."

"Good."

"As a matter of fact, Mark, everybody's here—including your wife."

"Tina is *here?*" He didn't mean to show quite so much surprise. More than a month ago he'd heard rumors about Tina and Bruce Scott. But he had guessed the affair was nothing more than a one-night stand. And he was hoping the weekend would be at least partly a vacation.

"Yeah," Shelby said apologetically, "she turned up with Bruce this morning. His people hadn't mentioned it, so we . . ."

"Don't worry about it. I'm just a little surprised they're still together. A month's a long time for Bruce." He chuckled. "For that matter, it's a long time for Tina."

"Well, I'm embarrassed."

Elliot clapped him on the shoulder and they moved toward the bar. "No reason. As I understand it, there are laws against discrimination.

There's nothing you could do about it anyway."

"She'll be at our table tonight. With Bruce."

It was one of the little things that Shelby's thorough planning hadn't taken into account. Elliot shrugged. "Well, that's show biz."

"McDade, you've shown me every damned thing in this valley and everything in this hotel except the most important thing of all."

"I don't think we've missed anything, Mrs. Shelby. What are you referring to?"

"The bar, for God's sake. Do you realize I haven't had a drink for more than six hours? That's unhealthy, McDade."

McDade wasn't certain it was part of his duty to entertain Mrs. Shelby beyond the guided tour. But the woman was quite forceful, and as they came in the front door he saw Mr. Shelby disappearing into the lounge just off the lobby. "Well, the fact is, Mrs. Shelby, the hotel has three bars."

"Which is the closest?"

"Uh, well, there is one right over there. But I would personally recommend the Skylight Room on the top floor. It has a beautiful view of the mountains."

"Okay, let's go. We can watch all those storm clouds gathering. What do you drink, McDade?"

"I occasionally have a small glass of sherry."

"Sherry? You mean that piddling little wine?"

"I rather like it, as a matter of fact."

"No, you don't. I'm going to teach you a few things about drinking, Mr. McDade. You ever had a Singapore sling?"

"I don't believe so."

"You'll like it, I guarantee it."

McDade frowned as the elevator doors slid shut.

"Did you see who just walked in?" the middle-aged woman said over the din of noise in the bar. "Mark Elliot!"

"Where?" her husband asked.

Tina Elliot had tried to ignore the crowd of people coming into the bar. They were obviously a group from one of the package deals offered by the hotel. They were asking about the prices of drinks, and whether or not they were included in the package, and then the wives were ordering stingers and whiskey sours while the men asked for beer. If the bartender hadn't just brought her a fresh drink she would have left immediately.

She was lifting it to her lips when the woman with the Nebraska voice said Mark Elliot had just walked in. Tina didn't drop the glass, or straighten, or even look in the direction the woman pointed. She took a long sip with her eyes fixed coolly on the bottles behind the back bar, then set the drink down. She shook a cigarette from her pack, calmly lighted it, then lifted her head and casually scanned the far end of the bar.

He was there, leaning against the edge of the bar and talking to Shelby, his head turned away. Tina gazed at the back of his head for a minute, then lifted her drink and slowly emptied it. She gathered her cigarettes and lighter and dumped them into her small purse. Then she slipped from the stool, squeezed her way through the crowd, and marched down the hall and out the side door of the hotel.

The wind was blowing harder now and there was a definite chill in the air. But Tina hardly noticed. Her head high and her mouth tight, she strode across the packed snow and down among the condominium buildings. When she reached the third one, she marched through the lobby and up the stairs. At the end of the hall she pushed a door open and stood glaring across the room.

"You son of a bitch," she said with controlled fury. "You dirty, miserable, lying bastard."

Wearing only his shorts, Bruce Scott was sitting on the couch examining a bruise on his left calf. He glanced over and smiled. "Hey, how's it going, baby? You been checking out all the bars?"

Tina stared at him for a minute, then slammed the door shut. "You knew he was coming, didn't you! You knew he was coming, and you didn't say a goddamned word!"

"Who?" He didn't look up this time, but there was a faint smirk on his face.

"Who? The great man. America's favorite host . . . the sweet, lovable funnyman with the forty zillion television viewers." Tina crossed the room and dropped into an overstuffed chair.

"You ought to be careful what you say

about your meal ticket, baby. Without that sweet, lovable funnyman, you might be back in Jersey slinging hash."

"You bastard. You knew he was coming all along, didn't you?"

"Well, now, for Mr. Shelby to pay me all that money to come here and slide down his mountains, he's got to get something in return for it. And to do that he has to have somebody to tell millions of people about this wonderful place, so they will come and pay his high prices. It's all business, baby, and to make it work, he's got to promote it. So I guess that's why he invited America's favorite host." He shrugged and smiled. "Maybe Johnny Carson couldn't make it."

"Johnny Carson my ass. I'll bet the whole thing is written in your contract."

"I don't mess with those things, baby; my agent takes care of them. I'm like a doctor; I never talk about money. I just count it very carefully at the end of the day. That's the way we professionals operate."

"Well, you've just ruined my holiday."

"Why? I noticed Shelby's ex-wife is here. It doesn't seem to bother him. You got to roll with the punches, baby. Elliot's just one man in your stable. Look at it that way."

"And I suppose you're figuring to make 'hot pants' Annette Colby just one more in your stable?"

"Hot pants?" He grinned. "I didn't know that. A sweet little ice skater like Annette? That's very interesting."

"Oh, God." Tina groaned and dropped her head back on the chair.

"Hey, baby, come on over here and give me a back rub, will you? I almost got killed out there on the slopes today."

"Rub your own goddamned back."

"Well, how about rubbing my front, then."

He was grinning at her, so goddamned sure of himself she felt like kicking him squarely in the groin. She rose and strode for the door.

"Hey, you mad at me or something?"

The door slammed and she was gone.

Scott rested his head back on the couch, then pulled himself up and went to the window. He sighed wearily as he watched Tina stomp her way back to the hotel. Then he studied the mountains and the sky just above them. The wind was really whipping the snow off the ridges now. If that kept up and a bad storm came in, he wondered if Shelby would call off the festivities. If he did, that meant fifty thousand dollars down the drain for Mr. Bruce Scott.

He had been a damned fool to let Shelby put that bad-weather clause in the contract.

He frowned as he studied the steep slopes about a thousand feet above the ski run. There was a hell of a big snow cornice up there. In France and Switzerland they always fired those things as quickly as they built up. But maybe this one was mostly rock, and in no danger of coming down.

"Enjoy your dinners, ladies and gentlemen," Shelby said into the microphone. "About ten minutes ago, a very charming lady asked me if this banquet and party were included in the package tour. I can assure you it is, and that is why you will see some of the people here being served McDonald's hamburgers."

There was laughter and some applause.

"No," Shelby went on, "we're going to treat you all first-class, because we hope that you will be buying condominiums and that you will be coming back to see us many times in the future. I will promise you this: everyone who ever comes into this valley will always be treated first-class. That's because I think you are all first-class people. That is why I have developed this resort, and why I have fought so hard to bring it to completion. Just remember this: if all the so-called environmentalists and nature-lovers had their way, none of you would be here tonight enjoying this mountain paradise. You'd be in a smoggy city, or in a crowded theater, or sitting home watching reruns of *Father Knows Best*.

"I am a nature-lover. But I am a man who loves it enough that I think it should be enjoyed by everybody. Thank you very much, and I hope you have an unforgettable evening."

The people came to their feet and cheered and clapped. Shelby grinned and finally lifted his hands to quiet them. "Thank you, but personally I'm ready for dessert. How about you?"

He was very good at a microphone, Caroline reflected—the calm, relaxed, confident leader. Maybe he should have a microphone permanently fixed to his chest.

"Very good, David," Mark Elliot said. The others at the table murmured agreement.

The place was filled to overflowing, with a couple dozen waiters squeezing among tables to deliver food and champagne. It was the noisy kind of half-social, half-commercial affair that Caroline hated. She ate only a few bites of her dinner, sipped lightly at her champagne, and hoped there would be an opportunity to make a graceful exit before too long.

To her left Florence Shelby suddenly leaned forward and frowned at Mark Elliot.

"Mr. Elliot, when you're on TV, is that whiskey you're drinking from that coffeecup?"

Elliot laughed. "No, I'm afraid it's coffee, Mrs. Shelby."

"That's disgusting," she said. Then she looked at her son's untouched dinner plate. "David, if you're not eating because you're worried about your waistline, look at Mr. Elliot. He's really putting it away and he's skinny as a rail."

Shelby smiled a little uncomfortably. "Sweetheart, you have an opinion on everything, don't you?"

"Yes."

"Mrs. Shelby"—Elliot chuckled—"I'd like to put you on my show."

Shelby snorted. "You do that and it won't be your show anymore."

Florence gave him a hard stare. "You set me up for that, didn't you?"

"I'm really looking forward to being on your show," Annette said from Elliot's other side. "You get such terrific action, and yet . . . you're so sweet with the people you talk to."

Elliot looked surprised. Then he smiled. "May I kiss you?"

She leaned a cheek forward and he kissed it. "And will you repeat what you just said tomorrow night?"

"Twice, if you like, Mr. Elliot."

On the stage, a five-man combo started a driving beat and two voluptuous girls came out performing a disco-style dance. Bruce Scott immediately pushed his chair back and came around behind Annette. "Dance?"

Elliot watched them go, then gazed silently at his wife. He knew the look on Tina's face very well—the cool, expressionless facade of unconcern. He also knew the fury and vindictiveness that was seething inside. She suddenly glanced across and caught his gaze. She quickly grabbed a cigarette from her case, and Elliot leaned over with his lighter.

"Thank you," she said coldly.

"Would you care to dance, Tina?"

She turned away and looked at the band as if she had not heard the invitation.

"Well, who'd have thought it!" Shelby suddenly exclaimed. He quickly signaled a waiter. "George, bring another chair."

Nick Thorne was squeezing his way through the crowd, now wearing a jacket and a turtleneck sweater. Caroline watched him, thinking he still looked out of place—as though he would rather be camping in a jungle somewhere.

"Come on over, Nick," Shelby called out as if he were an old friend.

Caroline smiled. "Hello. Glad you decided to join us."

"Join *you*," Nick said quietly.

"Champagne?" Mrs. Shelby asked.

Nick shook his head.

"Mother, this is Nick Thorne," Shelby said. "Nick, I'd like you to meet my mother."

"We've met."

"Yes, Mr. Thorne was shoveling snow out by your new house, David. He was showing us how the noise from the saws makes snowballs fall apart and tumble down the hill. It's a great trick."

Shelby ignored her. "Nick, this is Mark Elliot. And Tina."

Nick nodded. "How do you do?"

"Will you dance with me?" Caroline asked.

He was about to sit down, but he hesitated. "I'm afraid I don't know how to do that stuff."

"Then we'll make up something."

He smiled and drew out her chair.

"This is a pleasant surprise," she said as they moved through the crowd.

"Yeah, I'm a little surprised myself."

The dance floor was crowded, the older people paying no attention to the rock beat and the showy dancers.

Caroline glanced off as they squeezed onto the edge of the floor. "I think David is staring at me."

"I don't blame him. I think I'll stare at you too."

He was not a polished dancer, but he was smooth, and there was no question about who was leading. "You dance very well," Caroline said. "I'm amazed."

"Well, I don't want you to think of me as the wild man of the mountains."

"I rather like the thought."

"Then I'll wear a bearskin next time."

Caroline let herself go to the music, then glanced once more at David. "Huh!"

"What?"

"David is staring at Susan the way he stared at me."

"Does that bother you?"

"No. In fact it's rather liberating."

Nick smiled. "Your former husband does a great deal of staring."

The center of attraction on the dance floor was Bruce Scott and Annette Colby. He moved as if he were racing down the giant slalom course, and Annette followed along with equal enthusiasm, staying a little closer than necessary. Bruce touched her cheek and ran his fingers lightly down her neck.

"Have you ever had a really bad fall?" he asked.

She smiled provocatively. "Not since I was fifteen. A fantastic instructor taught me the art of falling."

"Did he explain that when you know you're going to fall and you're sure you can't stop it, then you just have to go with it?"

"Sure. He told me never to resist."

Mrs. Shelby refilled her champagne glass for the fifth time. "Aloha!" she called out as she held it aloft.

"Mother, this is *not* Hawaii."

"No? Are you sure, David?"

Shelby smiled uneasily and glanced at Elliot. "When she gets swacked, she always thinks she's in the islands."

Elliot smiled and lifted his glass to Mrs. Shelby. "I like it. Aloha!"

"See, David," she said, and clinked her glass to Elliot's. "You can't fool me. I always know where I am."

"But you had to decide how to land," Bruce Scott said. They were closer now, and he had a firm grip on her waist.

"You mean the position of the body?" Annette asked with mock innocence.

"Right. The position of the body is very important."

"I find it simpler on my back."

"Sideways is good, too."

"You fall sideways?"

Scott smiled and drew her tight against him. "It makes for a change."

The music ended and he held her close for another minute, his body still swaying gently.

"Perhaps we should find a more private place to practice our falls," Annette said, and pulled herself away. "In fact, I'm a little sleepy. I think I'll turn in early tonight."

Scott held her hand as they moved back. She guided him through a detour to where Cathy Jordan was sitting with her coach.

"Having fun, Cathy? You were doing much better with your spin today. I hope you don't have the same trouble you had in Toronto."

Leo quickly put his hand over Cathy's as Scott and Annette moved away. "Just spot and go, baby," he said quietly. "Spot and go."

Annette retrieved her purse from the head table. "Good night, everybody! I'm hitting the sack. Great party, Mr. Shelby."

Florence hoisted her glass. "Aloha!"

Annette smiled. "Good night, Mr. Elliot. See you on the show."

Bruce watched her move away, then felt a hard grip on his arm.

"Let's dance, honey," Tina said. "Or is your card all filled up with ice skaters?"

Scott smiled and looked off at the musicians. They were playing a hard-driving rock number now. "Sure, baby. I've been waiting all night for you to ask."

Shelby watched Nick Thorne as he seated Caroline and pulled back a chair for himself. Then he quickly rose. "Caroline? Shall we?"

"Are you sure you want to dance to that music?"

Shelby smiled a little stiffly and took her hand, leading her to the floor. "You interested in Nick Thorne?" he asked.

"He's interesting."

"He's also bad news for someone like you. You'll never get him away from the buffalo and the deer and the antelope."

"That's interesting too."

"I wouldn't like to see you pin your hopes on him."

Caroline almost laughed as David's secretary danced past with Gary Buckner.

"I'm funny?" Shelby asked.

"You are when you pretend to care about what I feel."

"Caroline, I do care what you feel."

"You care that I feel what you want me to feel."

66

It was a silly conversation, and it seemed to Caroline that they'd gone over the same thing a hundred times in one form or another.

"You're a lot more secure about everything these days," he said.

"I am more secure; I got a raise last month."

"I don't mean money. I mean you're more sure of yourself."

"I am. That's because I felt very unimportant next to you. After I left, I discovered it wasn't true."

"Do you work for David Shelby, Mr. Thorne?" Mark Elliot asked.

Nick was daydreaming, only half-watching the tangle of writhing bodies on the dance floor. He looked at Elliot and smiled. "No. I guess I'm what you'd call part of the local color. I built a cabin up here about six years ago. Long before Shelby decided to turn it into another branch of Disneyland."

Elliot chuckled. "Well, at least the value of your property has probably gone up a couple thousand percent."

"On the contrary, I think it's gone down about that much, Mr. Elliot. The place used to be very valuable to me. Now it's just another spot in a neon junkyard."

"Is that an opinion you'd care to express on nationwide television?"

"It's an opinion I've expressed to a dozen government committees, and to anyone else who would listen. Even to David's dear friend and staunch supporter Senator Maybrook."

"How did he take it?"

Thorne smiled. "I think he's having me investigated for 'un-American' activities."

Elliot laughed and lit a cigarette.

"Isn't it interesting," Thorne went on, "how all these people came up here because of the beautiful trees and mountains and fresh air and wide-open spaces? Then they pack themselves into a hotel dining room where the air is so foul with smoke they can hardly breathe? They want the quiet and serenity of the mountains, and then listen to this pornographic music that turns their ears into hamburger. And all the while they're drinking themselves into a stupor that will leave them with hangovers so big they won't be able to leave their rooms tomorrow. Then they'll all go home and tell their friends what a wonderful place this is, and what a good time they had in the wilderness."

"You know, Mr. Thorne," Elliot said, "I don't think I'd better have you on my show after all. You *are* un-American."

Nick laughed. "Maybe you're right. If this is American, I'm afraid I'm against it."

Elliot chuckled and turned away, and Nick watched the crowd again. In the midst of all the frenzied dancers, Mrs. Shelby was waltzing with McDade, swinging him around as if he were a rag doll. Nick watched them for a minute, then looked over at the little kid who had thrown the snowball in the parking lot that afternoon.

Apparently the boy's mother and father were off dancing, and the kid was trying to amuse himself. He had four or five champagne glasses lined up on the table and was circling around banging on the champagne bottles and plates and glasses with kitchen knives. He was keeping the same frantic beat as the drummer and musicians onstage.

Thorne smiled, and then winced as the boy's elbow suddenly hit one of the champagne bottles and sent it crashing onto the dance floor.

"Jason!" came the familiar cry. "For God's sake!"

Thorne decided he had seen enough of the revelry. He rose and touched Elliot on the shoulder as he moved away. "Take it easy," he said.

"Yeah, nice meeting you, Mr. Thorne."

5

◇◇◇◇◇◇◇◇◇◇◇◇◇◇◇◇◇◇◇◇◇◇◇◇◇◇◇◇◇◇◇◇◇◇◇

At the weather station just east of Grand Junction, Colorado, the man on duty made his hour entry into the log book. *Temperature 28. Barometer 39.54. Wind 24 knots.*

The barometer had been dropping for six straight hours now—considerably more than had been anticipated. It looked like there was going to be heavy snow in the mountains tonight, along with some strong winds.

He poured himself another cup of coffee and gazed out the window for a while, relieved that he had a good supply of firewood. The snow was swirling past so thick and heavy he could no longer see the tool shed thirty feet behind the building.

There were going to be a lot of people stranded in the mountains before the night was over.

Nick had skirted around the dance floor and was heading for the door when Caroline caught up to him. "Where are you going?"

"I think I'll escape."

"Can I go along?"

"There's nothing a fugitive likes better than company."

Nick retrieved his sheepskin jacket from the lobby while she went to her room for a poncho.

Earlier, when he drove up to the hotel, the snow had just begun to fall. Now it was coming down heavily and being buffeted furiously in all directions. Outside the door Caroline stopped for a minute and looked up, letting the flakes hit her face.

"Well, you got your snowstorm," Nick said.

"Yes, doesn't it feel good? I love it."

Nick laughed and took her arm as they headed for his jeep. "You might not love it if this keeps up."

"You really have a one-track mind, don't you?" she said when they were in the little car. "Are you really worried about the snow?"

He eased the jeep carefully along the slushy asphalt, reflecting that she was probably right. He had been crying wolf so long he was probably beginning to sound like the village idiot. "Do you know what corn snow is?" he asked.

"Corn snow? It sounds like something they would use in Hollywood."

Nick smiled and leaned close to the windshield to see past the splattering flakes. "It's just one of about fifty kinds of snow. It's little pellet-sized granules that come down like hail. If the temperature is low, they don't melt. They just form a layer, sometimes a foot or two thick, on top of the other snow. Then maybe you'll get three or four feet of soft snow on top of that layer, and as the temperature rises and falls every day, parts of that upper layer will thaw and then freeze into heavy slabs. What you end up with is hundreds of tons of very heavy snow resting on top of the corn snow, which is like a bed of dried beans. And if all of that is resting on a slope, the dried beans underneath are like roller bearings. When the weight gets heavy enough, suddenly the whole mass starts moving down the slope. Once it gets moving, it picks up everything else along the way, and that's what's called your class-triple-A avalanche."

"Corn and dried beans," Caroline said. "Sounds delicious."

"You wouldn't think so if you were at the bottom of the slope—which is where you happen to be in that hotel. And that's just one kind of avalanche. Some of the other tasty ones start when big overhanging cornices suddenly break loose from their own weight and just start snowballing down. When that happens, it can shake loose everything on the whole mountain range."

"How about glaciers? Shouldn't we be watching out for those, too? From what I've heard, some of them come roaring down at the rate of two or three inches every year."

"Ha ha," Nick said. His windshield wipers were going at full speed, but the snow was coming faster. Without chains, even the four-wheel drive didn't help that much on the slippery road. He found the turnoff, then gave it full throttle to keep his momentum through the last half-mile.

All Caroline could see when they parked was the faint glow of a light about twenty feet away. Nick circled the jeep and took a firm grip on her arm as they huddled against the flurries and moved to the door. Nick unlocked it, then checked a measuring pole before he came inside.

"Better than a foot since I left," he said, and shut the door.

The inside of the cabin surprised Caroline. With its rough-hewn logs and planked floors, it was primitive. Yet there was a feeling of solid comfort about it. A huge stone fireplace took up almost an entire wall, and several Navajo rugs were scattered about. Behind the living room there appeared to be a small kitchen, and a staircase rose from a corner. But the most striking features were the dozens of blown-up photographs hanging on the walls. Most of them seemed to be animals—stately-looking elks perched on rocky ridges; a ferocious mountain lion guarding her two cubs; closeups of small animals and insects.

Caroline removed her poncho and moved slowly around the room to study the photos. "Fantastic," she said. "They'd be almost too much if you looked at them stoned." She glanced at Nick. "You got any grass?"

"Sorry." He was reviving the fire with some small sticks.

"Ever use it?"

"No."

"Oh," Caroline said. She turned a complete circle, taking in all the pictures. Nick rose and brushed off his hands.

"Would you like a drink?"

"Yes. Thank you."

"I think there's some Scotch around here."

"Whatever."

He moved into the kitchen, and she heard cupboards banging.

"I think this elk is magnificent," she said.

"Yeah," he murmured.

"You have incredible vision. Great insight."

"Thank you."

She crossed to the stairs and moved up, studying the pictures on the side wall. At the top there was a small bathroom and then a huge bedroom that took up almost the entire floor. She moved inside and glanced at the jumble of camera equipment piled in a corner. Next to that was a small desk, and then what looked like a king-sized bed. Caroline gazed at it, then crossed to the window.

"Where are you?" he called from below.

She didn't move. Gusts of snow were splattering against the window, and she hugged herself, feeling cozy and comfortable for the first time since she had come to the mountains. She heard him coming up the stairs and then she knew he was standing in the doorway watching her. She turned and gazed silently at him. "We don't have very much to talk about," she said quietly.

He put the drink on the dresser as he came slowly across the room. Then his hands gently touched her waist and he drew her forward.

The kiss was light at first, no more than his lips brushing hers. Then he kissed her forehead and cheeks, and she felt her zipper slowly releasing as she slid her arms around his neck.

Tina Elliot moved unsteadily through the crowd and back to the head table, but she didn't sit down. She stood perfectly still for a minute and stared at the empty chairs. Then she squinted off at the stage and the singing guitar player. Bruce was nowhere in sight. She turned and headed back, wondering if he might have gone to the cocktail lounge for a drink.

She tried to remember if he had said anything the last time she saw him. They had danced twice. Then, while she danced with David Shelby, he was at the table talking to Mark. After that she had gone off to the ladies' room, and when she came back he was nowhere around.

He had mentioned that he was tired. Had he gone to bed? Or was he in the lounge? Tina staggered and caught herself as she moved across the lobby. On top of the cocktails before dinner, she had drunk far too much of that damned champagne. Breathe deeply, she told herself. If there was one thing she could do well, it was hold her liquor. She lifted her head high and walked smoothly into the lounge.

It was dark and crowded, but she squeezed her way to the bar and circled back, seeing no sign of him. He must have gone to bed.

She went to her room and got her parka,

moving steadily and purposefully. Then she went out the side door into the snow, smiling with anticipation. In Denver she had bought a pair of lacy black see-through panties and a matching bra, and she was wearing them now. Bruce was freaky for that sort of thing, and she had saved them for tonight. Her own desires had been stirring warmly ever since she dressed herself in front of the full-length mirror.

The snow was heavy, but the wind had died down a little. She was breathing heavily by the time she had slushed her way to the condominium. Once inside the door, she pulled off her boots and wool socks. She left them at the bottom of the stairs. Then, half-giggling to herself, she stopped on the staircase landing and dropped her parka, then pulled off the top and bottom of her pantsuit.

She felt silly and risqué, and suddenly very excited as she climbed the rest of the stairs and walked along the hall in the skimpy panties and bra. What if someone came out a door?

If it happened, she would simply smile and say hello and walk on. She giggled again, almost wishing it would happen.

Bruce's apartment was not locked, and she slipped in quietly. She moved across to the open bedroom door, and with her back to the hinges, she slunk seductively around. "Bruce, honey," she said softly. Then she stiffened, her eyes fixed on the bed. It was empty—not even mussed.

"You son of a bitch!" she screamed silently to herself. She flung the door open and

strode down the hall, the words echoing over
and over in her head. She ran down the stairs
past the landing and past her boots at the bottom, and out into the snow, stumbling onward
with blind fury.

She didn't notice the shadow ahead of her.
But suddenly it was directly in her path, and
she slammed into it, feeling hands grabbing
for her.

"Tina! Tina, for God's ..."

It was Mark. He was grasping her hair for
a minute. Then they both slipped and fell as he
tried to catch her wrists.

"Let me go!" she screamed as she went
down. She quickly scrambled to her feet again,
now free of him. She ran for the hotel, her
eyes closed.

"Tina!" she heard him cry mournfully behind her. Then she was through the door and
stumbling up the stairs.

The party was over by two o'clock. Those
who had accommodations in the lodge staggered up to their rooms, some with their wives,
some with other men's wives. The wind seemed
awfully loud as they closed the curtains and
prepared for bed. But they could see nothing
through the windows. The floodlights that normally lit the grounds had been turned off, and
there was only the intermittent battering of
driven snow against the side of the building.

For those who had walked or driven over
from their chalets and condominiums, the going was more difficult. Outside the front door,
maintenance men had shoveled away the snow

at midnight, but almost a foot and a half more had accumulated since then. The people laughed and held each other's hands and made their way down the steps. In spite of the harsh wind and the sting of snow swirling into faces, it seemed like great fun.

A group making its way toward the condominiums sang "Show Me the Way to Go Home," while a few of those going toward the chalets started a snowball fight, prompting a great deal of shrieking and laughter.

Those who were driving cars found it almost impossible to plow through the fresh layers of snow. Even with chains, the cars swerved and fishtailed and wheels spun and sent plumes of snow spraying out behind. Most of the drivers finally gave it up. They edged their cars as far off the road as they could and then trudged on through the snow-laden wind.

On the mountain slopes the wind tore at the ridges and whipped angrily at branches of pine trees. And the snow grew deeper and heavier, the freezing temperatures hardening the thick crust into lethal, thousand-ton slabs.

In some places there was slippage. A small overhang of accumulated snow would pass the point of equilibrium and drop to the thick blanket below. This in turn would move slightly, the added weight shifting the heavier mass a few feet lower on the slope. From beneath would come a rumble and a heavy grinding sound, and in the massive ice slabs one more fissure would be added to those that had been weakening its grip on the mountain through the last twenty-four hours.

The same thing was happening at dozens of places below the ridges. Beneath the roar of wind and the wrenching of pine trees, there were periodic thumps and rumbles, and the faint squeaking of stress as the huge frozen masses of ice and snow slowly shifted and the tension approached the breaking point.

Nick Thorne reached across to turn on the small bedside lamp. Then he looked at his wristwatch. Twenty minutes after five. He finally realized what had awakened him. Several muffled thuds came from somewhere outside, and for a moment the cabin vibrated.

After a glance at Caroline, he slid from the covers and hurried down to the front door. It was still snowing lightly, but the clouds had lifted and he could almost make out the tops of the mountains. Then he saw what had caused the thumping. In the long trough rising directly from his cabin, the snow was rough and tumbled, with jagged slabs of ice protruding from the mass. A small slide.

He frowned uneasily as he gazed at the surrounding mountains and the heavy mantle of snow that had accumulated during the night. Trees that had been clearly visible the day before were now huge lumps of white, and all the rough edges of the slopes and ridges were now ominously smooth—pregnant with the weight of new snow. My God, he thought as he quickly shut the door and hurried up the stairs, it was a miracle there hadn't been a hundred slides during the night.

In the bedroom he dressed quickly, putting on ski pants and parka, then laced up his boots. From the dresser drawer he got out the shells he had taken from Prentiss' truck and shoved them into a pocket. Then he gazed at Caroline for a minute.

He smiled, thinking about her request for grass the night before. And the Scotch he had fixed for her was still on the dresser. But she had done fine without it. She had been a very hungry girl when she got her clothes off.

Downstairs he put on snowshoes, then attached his skis to a backpack. When he was ready, he stood outside the door for a minute studying the long narrow trough.

He had been lucky. Bruce Scott had brought down a good amount of snow the day before, and that had eased the situation enough that this morning's slide hadn't been too dangerous. That's what Prentiss should have done with the whole mountainside twenty-four hours ago. He could have triggered enough small slides that the mountain would at least be partially stable.

It would be a long climb, and it might be too late now. But he had to give it a try. He trudged forward in the deep snow, adjusting his pack, squinting up at the masses of solid white hanging above him. If it could hang on for another four or five hours, he might be able to relieve some of the tensions.

"You think it was a success?" David Shelby called out from his private steambath.

"Everybody seemed to be having a good time," Susan answered.

The phone buzzed softly, and Shelby picked it up, at the same time looking out the window. "Yeah?"

"Mr. Shelby, the spectator stands at the ice rink have been pretty well torn apart by the winds, and the rink itself has a couple of feet of snow on it. But I think we can have everything fixed in time."

"Good. Anything else?"

"Some light fixtures down, and minor damage to shutters and so forth. Nothing serious."

"That's fine, Al, don't worry about it."

"And a lot of the guests' cars are stuck on the roads, blocking them up pretty much. Should we try to get them towed out?"

"Get the ice rink fixed first. I don't think anybody'll want to drive anywhere."

After he hung up he continued to look out the window for a minute. All the pennants and bunting had been torn from the buildings and were scattered around and half-buried in the snow. But the mountains looked beautiful. The pine trees were covered with frozen snow, and the slopes were all pure white and as fluffy as whipped cream.

"Here's your orange juice," Susan said, coming into the steamy room. She was wearing nothing, holding the glass between her thumb and forefinger as if it were some kind of medical specimen.

Gary Buckner must have been a very disappointed young man last night. After dancing with Susan until two o'clock he had suddenly found himself empty-handed, with Susan tell-

82

ing him good night and heading up the stairs with David Shelby.

But what the hell, Shelby had thought; there was nothing in Buckner's contract guaranteeing him a girl for the night, and he should have known better than to choose Susan.

"How about a kiss to go with the juice?" Shelby asked now.

She placed the glass next to the telephone and gave him a warm kiss, running her hand down his stomach. Then the telephone buzzed again. Shelby smiled and picked it up.

"Yeah?"

"Mr. Brenner is on the phone, Mr. Shelby."

Shelby grunted and motioned Susan out. "Yeah, Marty, where are you?"

"Listen, I'm in Denver, David, but they've canceled all flights up to the Rockies. Ed says we'd better not risk it with this kind of visibility."

"Marty, I don't give a damn about Ed and the visibility. I want you and that file here tonight."

"The roads are closed too, David. They say they probably won't have them plowed for another eight or ten hours. That's if the snow stops."

"To hell with the roads. We're talking about a ten-year multinational project, Marty, and you're telling me about bad weather? Offer Ed another five hundred bucks and see if that improves his vision."

There was a pause, and Shelby heard a weary sigh. "Okay, I'll try."

"Tell him the visibility up here is fine
—at least two thousand feet. Hell, I can even
see a little patch of blue sky to the west."

"Okay," Marty said, and hung up.

Caroline blinked curiously at the strange
animal. It was hanging upside down from a
branch and staring at her as if she were even
more odd-looking than it was. It was a two-
toed sloth, she finally realized—or at least a
picture of one—and it was hanging on the wall
only ten inches from her face. She smiled and
drew her arms from under the covers, then
rolled over.

Nick was gone. The pillow and blankets
were mussed, but there was no sign of him.
She listened for sounds in the kitchen below,
but heard none. "Nick?" she called.

She found a terry-cloth robe and went
downstairs. "Nick?" she called again. The living room and kitchen were both empty. She
opened the front door and saw the deep inden-
tation of footprints leading off toward the
mountains. She stared at them for a minute,
then quickly closed the door against the icy
temperature. My God, she thought, what kind
of a man was he to go for a walk in this kind
of weather?

She was desperately hungry. In the re-
frigerator she opened a package and found
two chunks of top-sirloin steak. There were
also eggs and a loaf of bread, and a half-gallon
carton of milk.

It was funny, she reflected as she turned
on the oven broiler. Generally she had no ap-
petite for breakfast. At best she had a glass of

orange juice, then slurped coffee until her one-
o'clock martini and lunch. It was amazing
what fresh air and wholesome lovemaking
could do for a person.

6

◇◇◇◇◇◇◇◇◇◇◇◇◇◇◇◇◇◇◇◇◇◇◇◇◇◇◇◇◇◇◇

Nick had almost reached the timberline. Even
with snowshoes it was tough going, and several
times the surface had broken, sending him skit-
tering down in a cascade of tumbling snow.
But he had trudged on, stopping for a brief
rest every fifteen or twenty minutes.

The clouds were growing dark again, and
the ski-patrol shack fifteen hundred feet above
was now scarcely visible in the descending
mist. But he knew there was a rifle there, and
somehow he had to get to it.

He paused for a minute, once more adjusting his pack. Then he looked across the face of
the mountain. Old Frown, the massive cornice
thrusting out from the mountain about two
hundred feet below the ridge, now looked twice
as large as it had yesterday. With the fresh
snow packed solidly around its sides and down
the front, it somehow didn't look quite so dangerous—as if it were now nothing more than a

87

huge lump protruding from the slope. But Nick knew better. The snow on the sides would provide no support, and since yesterday another thirty or forty thousand cubic feet of snow had settled on the top. That meant an additional five hundred tons of weight.

Below the cornice, the slope dropped almost vertically through the first two or three hundred feet. Then it eased off into a long steep run that ended squarely in the center of SkiHaven Village. How many cubic feet of snow and ice and frozen slab were on that slope? Nick didn't care to calculate. But if it ever started down, it would be like a dozen loaded freight trains racing side by side down a mountain.

He squinted up in the direction of the ski shack again, then pushed on.

Bruce Scott looked out the window as quickly as he got out of bed. It was gray and overcast, but it was no longer snowing. That was good. It meant the slopes would be hard and fast, with no melting slush to slow things down.

He ordered breakfast sent over from the hotel and then took a hot shower. He would have spent the entire night at Annette's place, but at three-thirty in the morning she had kicked him out. With all the photographers around, she didn't want the tabloid newspapers at every supermarket checkout counter displaying a picture of Bruce Scott coming out of her room.

"Your breakfast is here, Mr. Scott," a

voice called from the living room. He shouted "Thank you" and pulled on a turtleneck sweater, hearing the door click shut. Then, while he gave his hair a quick brush, he heard it click again.

"Good morning, darling. How do you feel?"

He frowned for an instant, then smiled. It was Tina. "Pretty good," he answered.

"Sleep well?"

He moved into the living room and gave her a quick glance as he strode past. She looked terrible. She was wearing ski pants and a sweater, but her eyes were baggy and her lips were chapped and wrinkled. He moved on to where his breakfast had been set out in the small alcove.

"How would you rate Annette?" Tina asked as she followed him. "I mean, on a scale of ten."

Her voice was still sweet, but the edge of nastiness was creeping in. Bruce pulled up his chair and emptied the glass of orange juice.

"Seven?" she asked. "Eight?"

He gave her a sour look and cut into his steak.

"Nine?" she asked, picking up an apple from the bowl of fruit. "My God, was she *that* good, darling? I don't think you even gave *me* a ten."

Bruce sighed and held the piece of steak in his fork. "Tina, either put that apple down or throw it at me, for Crissake."

She dropped it in the bowl and scowled. "It wouldn't hurt you enough if I threw it."

"Well, my ass hurts enough already. Jealousy's the biggest pain in the ass."

He had never seen her quite like this. Her face was flushed, and for a minute he thought she was going to cry. Instead, she suddenly reached across and grabbed his steak knife.

"Goddamn you!" she said, and leaned forward with the knife six inches from his face. "Stop behaving as if you can get away with anything! You son of a bitch!"

He glanced at the knife and took a drink of milk. He knew damned well she wouldn't touch him with the knife. Tina Elliot's opinion of herself was too low for her to ever take any drastic action. Deep inside she would already be picturing the police and reporters, and what the inside of a prison looked like. "Now, this is a real switch," he said with a smile. "You usually threaten to kill yourself."

If it weren't so damned pitiful, it would be almost funny watching her. She was livid with fury, but she couldn't move. There were tears forming in her eyes. "I'll rip you to shreds, you goddamned . . ."

Bruce picked up a piece of toast and spread marmalade over it. "Why can't you play it the way your husband plays it? He's got real style. You're pressing it, baby."

She still couldn't move. She was like a smoldering volcano that didn't have quite enough power to push the lava over the top.

"There's no point in threatening me, Tina. You've lost me. If you've got to kill somebody, kill yourself." He reached casually for the glass, but then his hand swung upward, flinging the milk squarely into her face. Then he had a firm grip on her wrist and he quickly pulled the knife away.

"You bastard," she whimpered. She covered her face and dropped into a chair. The tears were coming now. "You dirty bastard."

Bruce tossed his napkin into her lap. Then he lifted her by the arm and maneuvered her to the door.

"Tina, please..."

Through her tears she looked at him with a helpless, pleading sob, but he gave her the final push and shut the door firmly behind her.

"Christ." He sighed and returned to his steak.

Shelby called Caroline's room once more before he left his suite, but there was still no answer. He wondered about it as he went downstairs to the dining room. She didn't seem drunk the last time he saw her. But she must have slept somewhere.

Nick Thorne? Shelby tried to tell himself it was ridiculous. Caroline had more sense than that. Nick Thorne was one of those people who would never be content until he closed down every factory in America and every square inch of land was covered with grass. As for women, he probably liked them barefoot and pregnant, with lots of hair on their legs.

There were about a dozen people scattered around the dining room, and Shelby spotted his mother and McDade by the window. From what he had noticed last night, the two of them were getting along a lot better than he had expected. Except it looked like his mother was doing all the guiding.

Shelby asked a waitress to bring him a cup of coffee, and crossed to the table. " 'Morning, lady . . . McDade."

"You look awful, David. You should have eaten your dinner last night."

It was her standard greeting, and didn't mean anything. "You see Caroline this morning?"

"No. The last time I saw her she was doing the hunky-dory, or whatever you call it, with one of those young skiers."

"Isn't she in her room?" McDade asked innocently.

Mrs. Shelby gave him a long look and shook her head. "Really, McDade, you don't ask a man where his wife spent the night." She laughed and finished off her Bloody Mary.

McDade blushed and looked out the window. "It's a beautiful day, isn't it, Mr. Shelby? It's too bad the sun isn't shining."

"Did you know there's a man climbing the mountain out there?" Mrs. Shelby asked. "We've been watching him for an hour. He must be out of his mind."

Shelby squinted through the window, searching the slopes.

"Just across from that big lump of snow on the right," McDade said, and pointed.

Shelby finally spotted it, a tiny speck just below the level of the clouds. "Probably one of the ski-patrol men getting ready for the crowds."

"When does the skiing start?" Mrs. Shelby asked. From the look on her face, her only interest in the activity was to make sure she avoided it.

"A little after noon," Shelby told her. He quickly emptied his coffeecup and smiled. "Listen, I've got to go and get the festivities rolling, sweetheart. Want to come along?"

"What kind of festivities?"

"I'm going to work winter wonders, my darling. Want to watch?"

"What are you going to do—freeze the Red Sea?"

Shelby laughed. "For you, anything."

"But outdoors?"

"Next year, indoors."

"Then I'll wait till next year."

Shelby smiled and picked up their tab. "Don't drink too many of those things."

"Right on!" she said, and gave him a mock toast with the glass.

At the cashier's counter Shelby picked up the phone and dialed Mark Elliot's room. "Good morning!" he said heartily when it was answered.

Elliot sounded like a bear just coming out of hibernation. "Huh? Wha . . . who is it?"

"David, Mark. Rise and shine, old buddy. The big show is starting in about fifteen minutes."

"Oh. You mean the skiing?"

"No, but we've got dogsled racing, ice-boat racing, and speed skating."

"Oh. Well, I think I'll pass on it, David. I haven't even had breakfast yet."

"Listen, Mark, we can hold them up for a while. I mean, if you think your camera crew might be able to get through."

"No, no, don't do that. If I want any footage, I can have it restaged."

"Okay, but don't miss the skiing. We'll have the grand opening of the lift in about two hours."

"I won't miss it."

After he hung up he asked the girl for a telephone directory. The book was a skimpy little thing listing the Valley residents along with those in four or five of the closest towns. But there were no Thornes. He thanked the girl and went through the lobby and out the front door.

Most of the cars in the parking lot were buried under two feet of snow, but the plows were beginning to scrape the road clear. Shelby's blue Cadillac Seville was in the service garage off to the left, polished and still dry.

As he headed down the road to the dog-sled area, he felt his irritation growing. It was damned rude and inconsiderate of Caroline to walk out on him last night. And yet he knew it was partly his own fault. He should have told her yesterday that he wanted her with him all day today.

More than anything he had built the resort for her. It was his final effort, his supreme offering to effect a reconciliation. The whole thing was hers if she wanted it, and in return he wanted only that she become his wife again. God knows how he had tried everything else to make her happy—from diamonds and furs to one of the most fashionable apartments in New York. He had even tried to involve her in his work, having her put on cocktail parties and even act as his secretary on occasion.

He didn't know any other way to make a

woman happy. And as far as he could see, there were very few women in the world who wouldn't be ecstatic over the kind of life he had given her.

So what the hell did she want? A backwoods photographer who lived in an Abe Lincoln log cabin?

After their divorce he had hired a detective agency to watch her for a couple months, certain there must be another man involved. But they had reported nothing significant. She had gone to work for that magazine, working ten or twelve hours a day, and she seemed to go home and go to bed every night. Then on weekends she had dates with four or five different men, a couple of them who worked for the same magazine. But none of them appeared to be serious affairs, and as often as not she didn't even invite them in for a nightcap.

So what the hell was it? he wondered. Her talk about feeling independent and important didn't make much sense to him. What was so important about being an editor for a magazine that showed women all the latest fashions? And how much did she make—four or five hundred a week? Shelby sighed wearily and wondered if he was wasting his time even thinking about her.

There was a good crowd around the dogsled-racing area. Shelby fixed a big smile on his face as he parked the car and strode down the slope. There were also a number of photographers and newspaper people. He greeted them all before making a short speech.

It all went smoothly. After a few jokes he

fired the starting gun, and along with everyone else, cheered on the competitors. Then he presented the winner with a trophy, and drove down to the frozen lake, where he went through the same routine with the iceboat races. When that was over, he repeated the performance at the speed-skating races.

At the small airport outside Denver, Marty Brenner stood well away from the small airplane to have his last cigarette before takeoff. Ed Cavendish, the pilot was still over at the control tower, trying to get more specific information on the weather up at SkiHaven.

As far as Brenner was concerned, he didn't care if he ever saw the inside of that plane again, and he hoped Cavendish would come back shaking his head. Brenner didn't like flying in the first place, and he liked it even less in a little airplane with only one engine, and a propeller that looked like it should be hanging from the ceiling of some cheap Chinese restaurant.

In legal circles Marty Brenner was regarded as a feisty little attorney who was afraid of nothing, and was a master contortionist at bending laws to suit his clients' interests. There was some truth in the belief, and four years ago David Shelby had retained him for exactly that reason. Since then they had both prospered, and a lot of people who had fought them in courts had wished they hadn't.

The papers Brenner was now bringing to Colorado were a complex set of contracts drawn up essentially to throw a smokescreen over Shelby's dealings with Senator John Maybrook. Mostly they involved phony corporations and land sales funneled through third and fourth parties who were theoretically disinterested strangers. But a court or a couple of hard-nosed newspaper reporters would probably have no trouble untangling the can of worms.

So Brenner had no idea why Shelby was in such heat to have the papers up at Ski-Haven. Maybe he just wanted to show a few of them to the press with the idea they would be satisfied with the legitimacy of the deals. Maybe he wanted to burn them. In any case, when a client as profitable as David Shelby said jump, Brenner was inclined to respond. Except this time he wished he had said no, and that he was still in New York.

He finally saw Cavendish striding toward him from the tower building, and he dropped his cigarette and ground it out. Cavendish was shaking his head, but he was also walking with a determined step. It looked like bad news.

"They don't know a damned thing," he said when he finally arrived. "But I guess we could go up and take a look for ourselves."

"They don't know anything?"

"No. Half the telephone lines are down, and all they get is static on the radios. But there might be some open pockets up there."

Cavendish was a long, skinny man about forty, but he had that hungry look. The five hundred extra dollars Brenner had offered seemed to have made a deep impression. He squinted up at the sky now as if searching for a hole to go through.

"What if there aren't any pockets?" Brenner asked.

The man shrugged. "We can always come back." He gave Brenner a bland smile and headed for the plane. "Let's get going."

Nobody else was crazy enough to fly in such weather, and they had the runway all to themselves. Brenner slammed the door and buckled himself in. Cavendish then taxied to the end of the field and gave the plane number to the tower over his microphone. The raspy voice told them to go ahead and take off.

"Good luck," the man said doubtfully just before Cavendish switched off.

The noise from the engine was deafening. Then the whole plane shook and vibrated as they moved faster and faster down the asphalt strip. Brenner finally closed his eyes, saying a little prayer as they finally started to rise. Then Cavendish was yelling at him.

"What?" Brenner shouted back.

"You can smoke now if you want!" Cavendish said.

Brenner nodded, but didn't bring out his cigarettes. Instead he peered out at the farmhouses that were slowly shrinking beneath them. Then he looked up. He could see nothing in that direction. Fog seemed to be whipping past them as the plane suddenly tilted and they were going through a broad turn.

"You got any idea what direction you're going?"

"It'll be mostly instruments from now on," Cavendish yelled.

"Those mountains are pretty high, aren't they?"

"About fourteen thousand feet, some of them. I'll take us to fifteen."

Brenner supposed that made sense and that the thousand-foot margin made them safe. But he still would have preferred a clear view of the ground beneath them. He eased back and rested his head on the seat, then grabbed at the dash handle as the plane suddenly jumped and left his stomach behind. It was as if they were in an elevator going full speed to the fiftieth floor.

"Updraft," Cavendish yelled. "We'll be getting a lot of them, so you'd better hang on."

Christ, Brenner muttered to himself. What the hell was he doing here? He tightened his grip on the handle and closed his eyes. To hell with David Shelby. If he ever got out of this alive, he would give up all his high-powered clients with their big deals. From now on he would be an estate attorney and handle only little old ladies who drove electric cars.

Sometimes Nick could see the hotel and the village, and sometimes not. The clouds descended on him like a heavy fog at times, and he could scarcely see ten feet in any direction. Then a gust of wind would swirl past and he would be in the open again.

Through his binoculars he could see the crowd of people gathering at the bottom of the ski lift now—tiny antlike creatures wearing colorful clothes. As he recalled, Shelby was going to have some kind of ribbon-cutting ceremony, so it would be another half hour before the chairs started coming up. He trudged on, carefully placing a snowshoe into firm snow, then hoisting himself up another foot or so.

The ski-patrol shack couldn't be too far now. But the foggy cloud was obscuring everything a hundred feet above. He took another step and shifted his weight; then he gasped, flopping himself against the slope as the snow suddenly dropped from beneath him.

It was only a short slide—eight or ten feet—and then the settling mass suddenly stopped. Nick lay perfectly still against the slope, holding his breath for a minute. But there seemed to be no more movement.

He finally took a deep breath and started climbing again, now carefully testing the snow each time before he took a step. My God, he thought, there would be a hundred slides like that once those skiers started running down the slope. He wondered now if he could do any good with the rifle if he ever reached that shack. The whole mountainside was like a load of gravel in the back of a tilted dump truck. One little push in the wrong place, and the whole thing would be roaring down.

7

◇◇◇◇◇◇◇◇◇◇◇◇◇◇◇◇◇◇◇◇◇◇◇◇◇◇◇◇

Mark Elliot stepped up on the platform and shook hands with Shelby and Bruce Scott, then stood silently before the microphone. Several hundred people were gathered by the ski lift, and he waited while the noise level slowly diminished.

Only about half of them were wearing skis and were dressed for the slopes. The others were elderly, or were holding drinks, trying to numb their hangovers from the night before. To the left, Gary Buckner and a dozen other professional skiers were standing in a group, ready to go up once the ceremony was over. Tina was also there, her hands deep in the pockets of her parka, her face expressionless. Mark gazed at her for a minute, but her eyes were vacant, fixed on some remotely distant spot.

Elliot adjusted the microphone and smiled. "Ladies and gentlemen, welcome to Ski-

Haven. And on behalf of David Shelby, I thank you for joining us in christening this beautiful ski lift. For myself, I must apologize for the fact that my camera crew is not here as expected. But I understand that the roads are pretty well snowed under between here and Cedar Falls. However, I am sure they will be along shortly.

"We are indeed honored today by the presence of one of the world's most remarkable athletes, a young man who is well known on ski slopes throughout the world—from Fujiyama to the Matterhorn—and whose grace and skill, and more important, whose dedication to his sport has inspired a whole new generation and brought incredible beauty and meaning to winter athletics. I don't have to tell you who that young man is, of course. He is standing right here at my side. Ladies and gentlemen, Mr. Bruce Scott."

Elliot stepped back and applauded, and the crowd quickly responded with cheers and clapping. Bruce came forward with his arms in the air and gave them his best boyish smile.

"Mark, thank you. It's great to be here, and I've never seen more beautiful ski slopes. Let's get this thing started."

The crowd laughed as Shelby came forward with a huge pair of scissors and handed them to Scott. Behind them a broad red ribbon was tied between two posts, and Scott worked the scissors through the satin until the ends dropped. A roar came from the crowd; the machinery in the lift clunked into gear and the first of the empty chairs started moving.

Bruce Scott was surrounded by teenage girls as quickly as he stepped from the platform and started buckling on his skis. He finally rose and signed autographs, then smiled at the last girl in line. She was a voluptuous-looking sixteen-year-old wearing skis.

"Thank you, honey," he said as he handed her book back. "You want to ride up with me?"

The girl was speechless, as if Paul Newman had just asked her to dance.

"Come on," Scott said, and pushed off toward the gate to the lift.

The only autograph seeker left with an empty book was the small boy who had broken the champagne bottle at the party. Mark Elliot watched as he stared after Scott with a crestfallen look. Then the boy turned and skied off to the side.

"David," Elliot said into the microphone, "thank you for making all this possible."

"Thank you, everybody," Shelby responded, "for making all this possible. Have fun, and I'll see you all later." He stepped off the platform and headed for his car.

Gary Buckner moved to a position in front of the stand, a young woman ski jumper at his side.

"Ladies and gentlemen," Elliot announced, "Gary Buckner and Tracy Stevens."

The crowd applauded and the two moved off toward the lift.

In the figure-skating competition, Annette was the first to perform. She moved easily out on the ice, almost casually, as if there were no audience and she were skating just for the pleasure of it. Then, in the same relaxed manner, she began circling the rink, imperceptibly gathering speed until her cropped hair was ruffling in the wind and she seemed no more than a blur as she whipped past. With the tremendous speed she was suddenly airborne and twirling. The crowd gasped and then roared with approval as she returned to the ice on one foot and glided gracefully through a slow turn and into a camel spin in the center of the rink.

From there her program was an artful series of loops and spins and jumps, interspersed with ballet and contemporary dance steps. There were sensuality and humor, grace and artistry, all performed with a *joie de vivre* that enraptured the crowd. When she ended the performance with her arms upthrust and an expression of happy exuberance, they gave her a standing ovation. Even Cathy Jordan came to her feet and clapped.

Nick Thorne paused as he saw the empty chairs beginning to move along the suspended cables. The first four or five were empty, but then he saw the two dots of color appear. He watched as they moved slowly toward the first tower. Then he squinted upward into the misty fog and heavy gray clouds.

An airplane? The faint buzz sounded like that of a small plane passing over several thousand feet above. The sound grew louder as he listened. Then it seemed to linger, as if the craft were circling tightly through the clouds.

Nick wondered if the plane was supposed

to be part of Shelby's opening ceremonies, some kind of stunt flying, or a hot-rock pilot hired to buzz the hotel and the village when the skiing started. Or maybe it was dragging a sign that said "Buy Condominiums." Whatever it was, no pilot would be stupid enough to come down into this kind of terrain with zero visibility.

"P-twenty-three to SkiHaven control. Over."

For the tenth time Ed Cavendish took his thumb off the mike button and listened. There was still no response. "P-twenty-three to Ski-Haven control, over. . . . SkiHaven control, can you read me?"

Marty Brenner's stomach was beginning to drift sideways and up and down, sometimes seeming to float into his throat.

"Why in the hell don't they answer?" he asked in frustration.

Cavendish shook his head. "Either they don't hear us or they're answering and we can't hear them."

The worst part of it for Brenner was that he had lost all sense of direction, along with an inability to tell if they were going up or down, backward or forward. Through the front and side windows he could see only thick fog that seemed to swirl in every direction at once. At the same time the dials on the instrument panel flopped and quivered and made no sense at all.

"Maybe we just better head back for Denver," he said. He considered offering Cavendish five hundred dollars out of his own pocket if they could make it back alive. But he guessed that wouldn't set too well with Shelby if he heard about it.

"We could try to drop under this stuff," Cavendish said. "There's a chance it might be clear down there." He was banking the plane again, keeping one eye on the dials and the other on the swirl of fog, at the same time adjusting the throttle.

"You have any idea where the airport is?"

"It isn't exactly an airport. It's a small strip about two miles below the village. I assume Shelby had them clear off the snow this morning."

"Why do you assume that?"

Cavendish laughed and picked up the microphone again. "P-twenty-three to SkiHaven control. Over. Do you read, SkiHaven?"

Nothing but crackling static answered them.

"Mr. and Mrs. Courtney," Mark Elliot announced as the next couple came forward. "Mr. and Mrs. Courtney are patrons of the Colorado Cup, and themselves accomplished skiers."

Elliot watched as the woman waved to the small boy who had been unsuccessful at getting Bruce Scott's autograph.

"See you in a while, darling," she said. "Stay here and watch. You'll see mummy and daddy come down."

The boy looked even more lost and broken-hearted as his parents settled into the chair.

"Ladies and gentlemen," Elliot said into the microphone, "Mr. Shelby's very able people will gladly seat those of you who want to make the run with us. Thank you, and I'll see you at the top."

He stepped off the platform to where his skis were stuck in the snow. "Tina," he called out, and gestured for her to come over.

There was no doubt that she heard him. But by her contemptuous glance he might have been a bum trying to pick her up on the street. She gazed at the ski lift for a minute, then whirled and strode off toward the hotel.

He was a fool even to bother with her anymore, Elliot told himself as he buckled on the skis. He had gotten the same treatment last night after he picked up her clothes and brought them back to her room. He had knocked and called quietly to her for five minutes before the door finally opened. Then she glared at him, her robe buttoned tightly to her neck.

"I suppose you think I should thank you," she said, and grabbed the clothes.

"No, I—" That was as far as he got before the door slammed in his face.

The secret with women like Tina, he supposed, was to treat them like dirt. Apparently Bruce Scott had kicked her in the teeth last night. But if he gave her a little smile, or maybe a hard slap on the behind, he would have her back in a minute.

Elliot straightened and pushed off toward the lift, feeling a little awkward on the skis. The spectators seemed to notice it and gave him a round of applause as he stepped into position to catch a chair. He smiled and waved, then looked at the little boy standing off to the side.

"Son?" he called out.

The boy blinked uncertainly at him.

"You want to go up with me?"

His parents were in the chair ahead, about ready to be locked into the cable. The boy's mother looked back and glanced at the boy.

"Is it all right, Mrs. Courtney?" Elliot asked her.

"Well . . . yes, if he really wants to. Jason, would you like to go up with Mr. Elliot?"

"Come on, pal," Elliot said. "We might get up there in time to see Bruce take off."

The boy's face beamed. Then he dug in his ski poles and hurried over.

Three thousand feet above the ski lift, Marty Brenner felt a drop of perspiration skid down his ribs as he glanced over at Cavendish. They were dropping lower now, and suddenly there seemed to be a strained look on the pilot's face as he leaned forward and squinted out the window.

"Damn!" Cavendish said. He took a quick glance at the altimeter, but the plane continued its shallow downward spiral.

He was going to drop two thousand feet, he'd told Brenner. If they didn't get below the clouds by then, he was going to come up and head back for Denver. But they had dropped fifteen hundred feet already, and they were still locked in the endless shroud of moist gray. Brenner couldn't believe they were ever going to see clear skies again.

"You figure SkiHaven is right below us?" he asked.

"It damned well better be," Cavendish answered. He glanced out a side window and then yanked the stick back and kicked hard on the rudder pedals. Brenner grabbed the safety bar with both hands as the rear of the plane seemed to whip upward and then drop as they were buffeted from one side to the other.

"These damned canyons are full of winds and downdrafts," Cavendish muttered when he had the plane steadied again.

"You mean we're in a canyon now?"

"We're still above it, I hope." Perspiration was beading up on Cavendish's forehead. He reached over and gave the throttle lever a push, then eased the stick back a half-inch.

"To hell with it," he said. "This damned soup must go right down to the bottom."

Brenner relaxed a little as the pitch of the engine rose a notch. They slowly started to climb. Cavendish held it steady for a minute, straining to see out the window again.

The plane was vibrating now, struggling to lift them in the thin air. Then Cavendish gripped the stick hard as the buffeting came again, and the elevator was dropping them straight down. For a minute Cavendish didn't move. Then he pushed the stick forward and gave it more throttle. "Oh, my God!" he said.

"What's the matter?"

"The whole electrical mother's gone kaput!"

Brenner stared at the instrument panel, and at all the needles that had been jumping and vibrating a minute before. Now they were sagging to the side, motionless.

The plane had picked up speed in the dive, and Cavendish was drawing the stick back, pulling them out again. Outside, the foggy cloud seemed a little thinner, and beneath them there was a hazy whiteness.

At the ski-patrol shack Nick Thorne gazed up at the misty grayness above him and listened, not sure what to make of it. There was no question about the plane having dropped at least a thousand feet into the valley. At any moment he had expected it to break through the clouds and come gliding down over the lodge. But then it seemed to circle and suddenly the engine was laboring hard, as if they were trying to go up again. Then there was a brief sputter and it passed directly over his head, moving through the broad circle again.

Either the pilot was lost and trying to spot something visually to get his bearings, or he was having some kind of engine trouble. As the sound diminished and the plane seemed to be making a circle on the other side of the valley, Nick put the shells into the rifle he had found in the shack. Then he took off the snowshoes and buckled on his skis. The plane's engine was getting louder now as it circled back.

For the third time Cavendish banged his fist on the instrument panel. The needles jumped, but immediately flopped back on their sides. "It's no damned use," he said.

"Christ, can't we just go up?" Brenner asked. His heart was in his throat now, and with each passing second it was pounding harder.

"But which way is up?" Cavendish muttered.

Brenner had no idea. The plane was being thrown around so violently by the drafts, they were tilted one way and then the other as Cavendish fought the controls. It seemed like *up* was certainly straight above their heads. But from one instant to the next, that direction was different by ninety degrees.

"Christ!" Cavendish exclaimed as they were thrown upward. Then, just as abruptly, the floor seemed to drop out from beneath them. A minute later it was all over.

It came in a split second, but Marty Brenner had a clear picture of it. As the plane seemed to flutter straight down, Cavendish threw the stick forward and slammed at the throttle lever. And then they were suddenly out of the clouds.

Brenner was hanging onto the safety bar and looking out the side window at the same time. He saw a mountainside of snow dropping off below them, and farther down he glimpsed the lumps of pine trees sagging under their white blankets. Then, almost in the same instant, he saw the huge mass of white racing directly at them from the front.

Cavendish had started to scream, and he had pulled the stick all the way back into his lap. Brenner scarcely managed to get his mouth open before glass and metal and snow exploded in his face.

Bruce Scott didn't hear the crash. Along with three other skiers he had stood at the top of the slope listening to the circling plane for several minutes, and then he had pulled down his goggles and briefly studied the lower terrain before he pushed off. He was not even conscious of the shattering sound as he thrust his ski poles into the snow and let himself fly downward.

At the top of the ski-jump ramp, Gary Buckner was also concerned with other things. With freshly fallen snow, the slope below the ramp could be tricky for landing. If it was soft, he would have to bring his tips up at a sharper angle. If it was frozen hard, there was the danger of the skis racing out from under him. With these questions on his mind, the crashing thud sounded like somebody had dropped something in the hut, and for only an instant he had a flash of irritation. Then he was concentrating completely on the ramp, the three hundred and fifty feet of empty space he would soar through when he left it, and the slope of snow where he would land at sixty miles an hour.

He smiled as he crouched low and gathered speed through the first hundred feet. It was going to be a good jump.

Nick Thorne could hardly believe his eyes. The sound of the plane had come closer as it circled back from the far side of the valley, but Nick had almost lost interest in it by then. With the rifle loaded, he was scanning the lower slopes, trying to pick the most likely spots where he might trigger some safe snowslides. Then he was glancing off at the top of the ski run when the plane suddenly came into view.

It all happened so quickly, it seemed like an illusion. The plane was suddenly there, roaring out of the clouds, then it was slamming into the top of Old Frown. Fragments flew high in the air. Others skittered and cartwheeled across and disappeared in the deep snow along the surface of the cornice. Then there was a deathly silence, as if everything in the valley had suddenly frozen in place.

Nick looked off to where Bruce Scott had just started down the slope, then glanced at the colorful specks moving slowly upward in the lift chairs. Then he looked sharply back at the massive cornice high above them.

Was it moving? He stared, almost hypnotized as he felt the low, rumbling vibration in the mountain beneath him. The cornice *was* moving. The front two-thirds of it was slowly separating from the mountain, at the same time settling downward, pushing the softer snow in front of it. "My God!" he murmured under his breath.

It was as if it were all happening in slow motion, and Nick knew the whole mountainside was about to go. He was a hundred yards to the side of the cornice, but the ground beneath him was already vibrating and shifting from the massive movement.

Directly above him, chunks of ice were beginning to break away from the ridges now. Some of them were thudding to a stop just below, while others were beginning to tumble downward, bouncing, gathering momentum, starting more slides as they came.

He gaped at them for an instant, then flung the rifle aside. Moving fast, he dropped to the lower side of the shack, and as soon as he got there he grabbed tightly to one of the pine logs supporting the structure.

8

<<<<<<<<<<<<<<<<<<<<<<<<<<<<<<<<<<>>>

The hissing sound came first. Then the rush of
powdered snow roared past in a blinding fury
that tore the roof off the ski shack and sent it
spinning off below. An instant later the full
impact of the gathering avalanche hit. The
pine log was suddenly gone from Nick's grasp
and he felt himself thrown backward, then
bounced up. For a moment he was high in the
air. Then he was in the rush of cascading snow
again, twisting and rolling, being battered
from all directions by the swirling mass.

There was a final jolt as he came to a stop
a hundred yards below—his legs and hips
wedged tightly in the debris of snow and ice
and shattered lumber.

He held himself perfectly still for a moment, not quite believing he had escaped the
worst of it. Then he stared at the slope below.

The slide was still thundering downward,
picking up momentum as huge slabs of ice and

frozen snow cartwheeled and shot high in the air, some shattering with explosive bursts as they came down.

As Nick gaped across the valley, it seemed like every slope on the surrounding mountains was breaking loose. The hiss and roar of one would be drowned by another, and the ground beneath him rocked and shuddered with each thunderous cataclysm.

He twisted as hard as he could in an attempt to break free from the confining wedge. Then he began digging, hurriedly scooping out the softer snow and tossing aside the frozen chunks.

Gary Buckner experienced a strange sensation as he reached the end of the jumping ramp and thrust himself high into the air in the stiff, bent-forward position. It was as if a blast of powerful wind came up from beneath him at the same moment, and he felt himself sailing higher and farther than he had ever gone before. There was also a strange hissing sound coming from somewhere behind him. But he kept his eyes fixed rigidly on the landing slope far below, and as the moist wind tore at the exposed part of his face, he realized he was going to overshoot the four-hundred-foot mark by at least two hundred feet.

He couldn't believe it. The world-record ski jump was five hundred and seventy-seven feet, and he would still be high in the air when he soared past it. And his form was faultless, his nose almost touching his skis as he leaned far forward, his arms tight against his sides.

And then he saw it—the thrashing river

of snow racing down beneath him at twice his speed. For a moment he couldn't believe his eyes; it was like a grotesque nightmare. But then he heard the deadly rumble from behind and he knew where the blast of wind had come from. It also explained why he was sailing so far over the landing slope.

For a moment he held himself steady, almost paralyzed by the sight of the churning snow and crashing ice slabs beneath him. Then he screamed, hearing no sound come from his throat as he spread his arms and legs and began flailing at the air as if his struggling might stop his rapid descent into the roaring maelstrom.

His back struck first. Then the earth seemed to leap beneath him and he was thrown into the air for a moment, a huge slab of frozen snow whirling past. Then he was into it again, tumbling, sliding, buried in the moving snow for a moment, then thrust up and slammed by a heavy boulder.

For an instant he saw a house in front of him. Then there was a wrenching crash and he seemed to be whirling onward in a thrashing jumble of boards and timbers.

It seemed like an eternity, but it finally stopped. There was still roaring and hissing, but it was from other slides, and he was no longer moving. He was stretched out on his back, his head lower than his feet, and in the sudden stillness a cloud of fine, misty snow settled quietly down on him.

For a minute he stared at the ceiling of heavy gray clouds above. Then he felt the sharp pain in his upper back, and his legs seemed to be twitching uncontrollably. He moved an arm and tried to lift his head, but then dropped it back. A moment later he felt nothing in his unconsciousness.

Bruce Scott was aware that something was wrong almost as quickly as he made his first jump turn. The hissing sound and the sudden blast of wind that hit him were the same sensations he had experienced less than twenty-four hours earlier. Except, this time they were much closer and far more powerful.

With one glance he verified his worst fears. Less than two hundred yards behind him it looked like somebody had set off a huge charge of dynamite. Great chunks of frozen snow were hurtling in the air, while a cloud of misty snow mushroomed up from the slope.

He took no more backward glances, and this time he knew that the trees would give him no protection even if he could reach them. The packed snow beneath his skis was already beginning to vibrate and shift, and with a desperate heave he drove hard with his ski poles and crouched low, heading straight down the forty-five-degree slope.

Only some kind of miracle could save him. The avalanche might clog and dam itself halfway down, or a rocky ridge might slow it a little. But Scott knew better than to count on it. He had no more faith in miracles than he did in tooth fairies or virtuous women. This time he was not going to escape. He suddenly felt the blast of compressed air from behind; he was being blown down the hill now, and his skis were beginning to slither out of control.

Ahead of him there was a small rise that he normally would have avoided by circling to the left. But there was no time now. He crouched lower, his ski poles tucked under his armpits, then thrust himself upward as he reached the crest of the rise.

The wall of snow struck him in midair. For a moment he was engulfed in the thrashing snow and ice, all of it flying twenty feet above the surface of the slope. Then his ski tips hit and were torn from his boots. He was facedown the next few seconds. Then the rushing mass was tumbling over him, and he was deep within it, being pummeled from all sides as it continued the mad race down the hill.

It seemed as if it went on forever, twisting and hammering his body, then compressing it more and more as he finally tumbled to a stop and more snow came crashing down from above.

Then, finally, there was silence.

He was in an almost upside-down position. But he was frozen there, his arms and legs packed solidly in place, and no more than two inches of air in front of his face.

His heart pounding, he breathed deeply for a minute, scarcely believing he was still alive. He could still feel the shuddering, and he could hear the muffled thunder of more slides on the mountain. But he was no longer moving.

It was hard to determine if any of his bones were broken. They were all bruised and battered, but he couldn't move them enough to feel any breaks.

After a minute he tried to turn his face up by pressing his forehead against the snow.

He partially succeeded, gaining another inch or two of breathing room.

How deep was he? From the tiny bit of light that was filtering through, there had to be at least thirty feet of snow above him. His right hand was less than ten inches from his face and he tried to pull it closer. It moved no more than an inch.

He twisted the hand and worked the fingers, scraping at the packed snow. A little of it was breaking away, and he continued working at it, doing the same with his left hand.

My God, he thought, was there a chance at all of his being rescued? And how many other people were buried in the debris? He felt his heart pound a little harder as he thought about it. Buried this deep, he would be the last person to be found.

He had to stay calm, he told himself. If his heart beat too fast, he would use up what little oxygen he had. He had to breathe easily and not panic. Just keep working with the fingers—slow and easy.

Mark Elliot and Jason Courtney were only halfway up the lift when they spotted Bruce at the top of the slope.

"Well, at least we'll have the best seats in the house for watching him," Mark told the boy.

By then they were passing one of the highest towers, and Jason leaned over to peer at the ground a hundred feet below. Then he squinted up at the gray ceiling of clouds.

"Do you think that airplane is lost, Mr. Elliot?"

Mark hadn't paid much attention to the buzzing and sputtering overhead. "I wouldn't think so," he answered. "They're probably tracking him on radar down at the airport, guiding him in for a landing."

"Huh. Sounds like he's going around in circles." Jason looked at his parents moving along in the chair ahead of them, then waved when his mother twisted in her chair and smiled back at him.

Mark's eyesight wasn't good enough to make out what Bruce Scott was doing at the top of the slope. He glanced up as the sound of the airplane seemed to pass directly over them.

"There goes Bruce," Jason said at the same time.

Mark looked, watching the tiny spot of red drop down the slope. Then he squinted at the mass of snow higher on the mountainside. He wasn't sure, but it seemed like a shadowy form had appeared and disappeared up where the clouds were butting against the snow.

"Gee, look at him go," Jason said. "He's coming straight down now, not even making any turns. Boy!"

Mark sensed something was wrong. Then the chair suddenly jerked and stopped moving.

"Mr. Elliot, what's—?"

"Oh, my God!" Mark breathed. He could see it then; a huge mass of writhing, churning snow was racing down the slope just behind

121

Bruce Scott. Within it, flat chunks of snow fifty feet across were sliding along, then tumbling, some of them shooting high in the air. The sound was even more terrifying. The hissing sound was joined by a rumble, and then a growing roar that was almost deafening. Mark and the boy watched speechlessly as the deadly wall rapidly overtook Bruce Scott. Scott was crouched low, and then he suddenly flew into the air from the crest of a small ridge. An instant later he was gone, enveloped in the rush of white.

"Mom!" Jason screamed, and suddenly moved forward as if to dive out of the chair. Mark grabbed his shoulder and held tightly, gaping at the slope directly above.

The ski-lift towers were dropping one by one, some of them uprooted, others slammed to the ground, others disappearing completely as the onrushing snow thundered and hissed.

A look of anguished terror came to Jason's face as he watched his mother's and father's chair suddenly torn from its connecting bar. Arms and legs flailing, they seemed to explode out of it, and then they were being swept away in the torrent.

With one arm tightly around the boy's waist, Mark gripped the connecting bar above them and closed his eyes as the impact came.

At the ice rink, Cathy Jordan was pleased with her performance. Annette had brought the house down with her effervescent manner and a routine that had a great deal more exuberance than it did technical excellence. But so far Cathy had done everything close to perfect, and as she skated gracefully around the perimeter of the ice and moved toward the center for her spin, she knew she had the Shelby Cup if she didn't falter.

Spot and go, she told herself. It was the same thing Leo had been pounding into her head for the last twenty-four hours, and she was determined not to let anything else enter her mind.

She eased her speed slightly, then tightened her turn and was ready. The spot she picked—the imaginary anchoring place for her eyes as she whipped her head around—was a snow-covered pine tree fifty yards away and a short distance up the side of the mountain. She fixed it clearly in her mind and then swung smoothly into her spin, steadily gaining speed as the pine tree flashed in front of her like a fluttering movie film.

And then the pine tree suddenly disappeared in a whirling white mass. But she still knew the spot, and her spin was perfectly balanced. She felt as if she could go on for hours, and for the first time in her career she added a new facet to the routine. She gracefully lifted and lowered one arm and then the other, at the same time increasing her speed.

On the judges' platform, David Shelby was one of the first to see the approaching avalanche. While Cathy was performing he had glanced up, hoping to catch a glimpse of Bruce Scott making his run down the distant slope. Then he had stared for a minute, uncertain what he was seeing.

The entire slope of snow beneath the ski-jump ramp seemed to be moving. The ramp itself was lifting, then buckling and twisting, then disappearing in a huge cloud of exploding snow. He glimpsed a jumper flying through the air for a moment. Then the man was plunging into a churning mass of snow and being swept away. Farther on, at the free-style ski slope, the same thing was happening—a torrent of boulders and ice slabs and tumbling snow careening down the mountain.

And then he heard it, the deadly sound just above them. Hissing, rumbling, and then the shuddering roar as snow and ice erupted from the onrushing mass.

People in the stands were screaming now, piling over each other to get out. "Jesus Christ!" one of the judges next to Shelby exclaimed. His chair clattered away as he jumped from the stand and ran. Shelby also ran. He was seated in the chair farthest away from the slope, and he was off the end of the stand in one bound, and then racing through the parking lot.

"Cathy!" Leo screamed from the edge of the rink.

She *must* have seen the avalanche coming. But she continued to spin, her arms rising and falling. "Cathy!" he screamed again. But he knew it was impossible for her to hear him over the other screams and the roar of the avalanche. As he screamed, he ran for her. Then the cloud of whirling snow swept over them. With his hand grasping her forearm, they were suddenly slammed to the ground and then lifted and slammed down again as they were swept along in the deluge.

At Nick Thorne's cabin, Caroline had taken a long leisurely shower after breakfast. When she was dressed again she found a huge pile of Nick's photographs in a closet. She took them downstairs, and with the radio playing country music on the only station she could find, she went slowly through the pictures imagining how some of them could be used in fashion layouts.

It was almost noon when she finished. She looked out the window at the mountains, wondering where he had gone, and if he had any intention of coming back before night. Then she went to the kitchen and made a sandwich and a fresh pot of coffee.

She was standing at the window with a cup in her hand when the radio suddenly crackled and went silent. She reached across and turned the dial several times, then switched the volume knob on and off. Still there was no sound at all, as if it had been unplugged.

It was odd, she reflected, and then she felt the cabin quiver. An earthquake was her first thought, and she stood perfectly still, waiting for the heavier jolt. Instead, the vibration seemed to grow steadily stronger. Then she heard the rumbling sound outside.

She still thought it was an earthquake as she stared at the high ridges of the mountains. Huge chunks of ice and snow were tumbling down, and a great white cloud of powder seemed to be drifting up from the slopes. And then she saw the tumbling ice cakes and the surge of heavy snow racing down the mountainside.

The ski-jump ramp seemed to lift from the mountain for an instant. Then it buckled and was sliding down and disappearing in a swirl of tumbling white boulders.

Just to the left of it another slide began, then another several hundred yards on the other side. A moment later the whole mountainside seemed to be sweeping downward and disappearing into a cloud of swirling white dust.

Caroline held her breath through a full half minute. Then she looked sharply at the long vertical trough just above the cabin. There appeared to be no movement in it. But in the cabin, dishes were still rattling, and several of Nick's pictures dropped from the wall. She quickly put her coffeecup on the table and got one of Nick's parkas from the closet. My God, she thought, was Nick up on that mountain? She suddenly became frightened as she hurried out the door and headed for the hotel.

Nick Thorne finally worked the snow away from his legs enough that he could pull them out. Then he moved a few paces across the slope, making certain none of his bones were broken.

How many people had been killed, he wondered, and how many more were trapped under the snow? He felt a little sick as he gazed into the valley. The hotel was still standing, but one side of it had settled several feet. It looked as if the avalanche had knocked it from its foundation and filled most of the lower floor with snow.

The village also had been hit. Half the buildings were now scattered across the lower end of the slide, no more than splinters now. Nick could see people running, some fleeing from the mountain, others scrambling over the snow to help the victims.

The ice rink was gone, buried under at least fifteen feet of snow. In the parking lot behind it, the avalanche had covered half of the cars before it had stopped.

On the slope about thirty feet below Nick, the heel end of a ski was sticking up at an angle. He made his way slowly down the incline, dropping almost to his waist a couple times as he hit soft spots.

When he reached the ski he yanked at it several times and finally got it out. It was whole, and the binding was still intact. He quickly buckled it on, then headed across the snow at a shallow angle. The lumpy terrain and the protruding slabs of ice made the going difficult on one ski. He made a sharp turn, avoiding a deep chasm, and then brought himself to an abrupt stop as a sudden explosion shattered the air.

There was no doubt about where it had come from. A white cloud suddenly appeared over the hotel, raining down bits of ice and snow. Gas! Nick winced as he saw more people running. Then he pushed off again, taking a steeper course down the slope.

Florence Shelby rose to her hands and knees and looked around the dining room. "McDade?" she called out.

The room was almost dark, and she squinted off at the corner. "McDade, are you all right?"

"I think so, Mrs. Shelby." His head came over the edge of a toppled table, and he rose cautiously. "Are you all right?"

"I lost my drink!" She pulled herself to her feet and brushed loose snow from her dress. "God Almighty, what the hell was it?"

"I think it was an avalanche."

There was no longer a wall on one side of them. It was now a solid bank of snow that extended halfway into the room and blocked the door to the lobby. The other half of the room was a tangle of chairs and tables, and the big window was now packed to the top with snow. But it was still intact.

It had all happened so fast, Mrs. Shelby still wasn't sure what had hit her. At one moment she had been lifting a Bloody Mary, and then she was staring into her glass, wondering why the ice cubes were rattling. Then she realized the whole room was shaking, and she looked out the window. What she saw was a mountain of snow crashing through the condominiums, flattening them like cracker boxes, throwing some high in the air. Then, in what seemed like a split second, the white mass was across the terrace and slamming into the dining-room window. Then she was flat on her face with her head squeezed between two overturned tables.

In La Jolla she had occasionally looked at

the Pacific Ocean and wondered what a tidal wave would look like. Now she knew. Except this one had been pure white and came down a mountainside.

She didn't think she had any broken bones. But there was a lump on her head and a little blood trickled down her fingertips when she touched it.

"That fellow was right," she said as Mc-Dade pushed through the furniture toward her.

"What fellow?"

"That photographer. The one who showed us how the snow breaks up."

McDade finally reached her. "You're hurt."

"It's just a flesh wound, as they say in the movies. Is there any way we can get out of here?"

"The kitchen door is over there, if we can get to it."

"Lead on, McDade."

He took her by the hand and pushed furniture aside as they squeezed through. At the door they both yanked on a table in an effort to clear the way.

"What's that smell?" Mrs. Shelby asked.

"I don't know."

"I think it's gas, McDade. The pipes must have broken."

The table finally came loose, and McDade pushed open the swinging door.

"Get back!" a voice screamed from the kitchen.

They both saw it. The chef was up on a chopping block, reaching for a broken tangle of electrical cable that was hanging loose from the ceiling. The wires were spitting out red and blue sparks, and the man waved them off as he tried to grab the wires. "There's gas in here!" he yelled.

McDade let the door swing shut. He had just turned to Mrs. Shelby when the explosion came.

9

◇◇◇◇◇◇◇◇◇◇◇◇◇◇◇◇◇◇◇◇◇◇◇◇◇◇◇◇◇◇◇◇◇◇◇

Tina Elliot was wearing the black bikini panties she had bought for Bruce Scott. Other than the T-shirt with the word BRUCE across the front, that was all she was wearing, and she lay silently on the bed, her eyes closed.

She hadn't noticed the avalanche, nor did she feel the explosion that rumbled through the hotel. She was breathing shallowly, her numbed hands occasionally twitching from the oxygen-starved nerves.

After she strode away from the ski lift she had gone directly to the hotel and back to her room. On the dresser there was a quart bottle of Chivas Regal, and she had filled a water tumbler and then emptied it in three long gulps.

"Don't ever take those pills after you've been drinking," the doctor had told her when he handed over the prescription last week. "There are probably more accidental deaths from mixing alcohol and sleeping pills than from any other cause. So be careful, Mrs. Elliot."

After she finished the Scotch, she dumped all twenty-four pills into her palm and washed them down with a couple more swigs directly from the bottle.

She almost vomited when she finally got them down. But she breathed deeply and closed her eyes, and after a couple minutes the nausea was gone. When she lay down on the bed, she was overcome by a pleasant sleepiness and a feeling of euphoria.

She was really not angry with Bruce, she decided after a while. Nor did she hate Mark. She'd had good times with both of them, and the way things had worked out, it was probably more her fault than anybody's.

It occurred to her then that she should write a note. She should tell both of them how much she loved them, and how silly she had been to be jealous. Yes, she would write a note. But she was too sleepy right now. She could hardly lift her arm. It was all tingly, and her hand felt numb.

Later. She would do it later.

She was having a strange dream in her half-sleep. There was a great deal of muffled hissing and roaring, and for a minute the bed seemed to quiver. Then she was completely asleep.

Shortly after the explosion shuddered through the room, the phrenic nerve controlling her diaphragm began to pulse erratically. Finally, completely deadened by the drug and the alcohol, it ceased to function and she was no longer breathing.

"Can anybody hear me?" Bruce Scott called out. He closed his eyes and listened, breathing heavily from the effort.

He had finally managed to scrape enough snow away so that he could bring his right hand to his face, and he had dug out a little more breathing room. But the snow was covered with blood from his torn fingers.

"Can anybody hear me?" he shouted desperately.

Dangling sixty feet above the snow, Mark Elliot wasn't sure how much longer he could hang on. He was gripping the vertical shaft with both hands, and the broken coupling just below his grip provided a little more traction. But Jason was clinging tightly to his back, one arm around his neck, and the added weight was already bringing painful aches to his arms. "Can you climb up a little, Jason?" he asked. "If you could reach the shaft and get your feet up on my shoulders, it would take some weight off my arms."

He could feel the boy shift, and he knew Jason was looking down at the sloping snow far below them.

"I'm afraid, Mr. Elliot."

"Okay, Jason. Just don't look down anymore."

Elliot twisted his head and moved his dangling legs around, trying to feel what was left of the shattered chair just below them.

There seemed to be some steel rigging, but it was swinging freely and there was nothing he could grasp between his feet for support. He finally gave it up and closed his eyes, praying he could hold on until someone came to help.

In a way, he supposed, they were lucky. There wasn't much doubt that everybody else on the lift had been swept away and was buried by the avalanche. But for some reason the tower just ahead of them had not toppled, and the one behind had been protected by enough trees that the sweep of snow had been partially deflected. The miracle of it was that the torrent of flying slabs and boulders had not knocked them out of the chair when it hit. But at the last moment they had both instinctively come to their feet, trying to get higher, Mark clinging to the shaft and Jason hanging on to his legs through the shattering bombardment. Then it was suddenly gone, and they could hear the roar and crash as it continued on down the slope.

Jason had managed to inch his way up and get an arm around Mark's neck, but now he would go no farther.

Mark listened, hoping to hear voices, somebody shouting up to them. He could hear only his own heavy breathing and a quiet whimpering from Jason.

He finally opened his eyes and looked up. The shaft he was clinging to was about eight feet long and hooked into the sagging cable directly overhead. There was a second, smaller cable tangled around the hooking mechanism —the broken end of it dangling a few feet above his head. He wondered if that was the power cable, and if it was alive. But the electrical connections must have all been cut by the avalanche.

He tried to shift his grip and ease the strain a little. Then he closed his eyes again, listening. There was only the wind, as if there was no longer a living soul in the entire valley.

On the single ski, Nick crouched as low as he could and flew down the slope, turning and twisting to avoid the roughest areas, sometimes scraping his left boot along the snow to keep his balance. Then he suddenly turned the edge of the ski sharply against the slope and plowed to an abrupt stop.

Off to his left somebody was buried almost to his armpits, trying to dig himself out. Nick quickly pushed off and glided to the man's side.

"Prentiss! What the hell are you doing up here?"

"Checking," the ranger said. He gave Nick a sad look, as if he knew how foolish it sounded.

"Alone?"

Prentiss shook his head. "No . . . Ralph's . . . he was swept away."

Nick nodded, then helped scoop away the powdery snow that had the ranger trapped.

"My God," Prentiss breathed when he climbed from the hole and looked down the slope. "They were just starting the figure skating when I left. There were a couple hundred people in the stands."

Nick grimaced and got out his pocket binoculars. The ice-rink area was covered deeply with snow. He could see some colorful stocking caps, and what might be arms and legs protruding from the debris. In the parking lot people were still struggling to free themselves.

"Can you get down there?" Prentiss asked. "I'll go to the hotel."

"Are you all right?"

Prentiss was favoring his left leg, but he nodded when he got his skis back on. "I can make it."

Nick put the binoculars back in his pocket and pushed off, angling down toward the ice rink. For the first time he thought about Caroline, wondering if she had stayed at the cabin this morning. He hoped to God she had.

McDade finally gave it up. The debris from the explosion in the kitchen now made their escape in that direction impossible. He'd finally wedged the door open and cleared away a huge table that was jammed against the opening. But beyond that there was a solid wall of broken timbers and studding and plaster that had dropped down from the upper floors. "It's no use." He sighed, then squeezed his way back to the dining room.

Mrs. Shelby had made herself as comfortable as she could, sitting under the keyboard of an upright piano. If the hotel was going to collapse on them, at least she would have some protection there.

"Terrific," she said dully. "So what do we do now?"

"I don't know." McDade brushed himself off and sat down on the carpet next to her.

"Do you think there's anybody alive out there to help us?"

"Oh, I'm sure there is. It's just a matter of time before they start digging."

Mrs. Shelby sighed and opened her purse. "Well, we might as well enjoy ourselves." She put a cigarette in her mouth and lifted a lighter to it. Then both the cigarette and lighter went flying across the room as McDade slapped at them.

"What the—?"

McDade smiled apologetically. "Gas."

"I thought it already exploded."

"It exploded once, but it's still leaking. Can't you smell it?"

The three fire trucks had first tried to go around the north side of the village to reach the access road to the hotel. When they found that was blocked, they circled back and moved directly through the main street. Then, sirens blasting, they joined the ambulance and the rescue truck that were making their way slowly along the icy road.

The biggest problem was the parked cars on both sides of the road—sometimes making the gap too narrow for the larger vehicles to squeeze through. With the ambulance moving far ahead, the driver of the lead fire truck finally gave up trying to avoid fenders. He gunned the engine and bulled straight through, jolting the cars aside in a crash of wrenching metal.

They were all moving fast, sirens blaring, when the secondary slide hit. In the lead, the ambulance driver saw it coming. He had just rounded a corner that curved through a cut in the mountain, and he saw the mass of snow sliding quietly down the slope toward the road a hundred feet ahead.

He hit the brakes, but nothing happened. The ambulance swerved and fishtailed, but continued gliding across the ice directly into the path of the slide. A moment later the tumbling snow picked it up and silently deposited it fifty feet to the side of the road.

Behind it, none of the other vehicles were able to stop. With the sirens still blaring, the rescue truck skidded sideways into the snowbank. The first fire truck slammed head-on into it, and the others jackknifed into the pile from behind.

In the parking lot next to the ice rink, David Shelby did what he could to help dig people out of the snow. About half of the spectators had escaped the worst of the snowslide. Some of the others had been knocked down and were suffering from broken arms or legs, or were just banged up. Most of those who had not been hurt were now helping to dig. But at least the panic had subsided, and things were getting organized.

When he had first driven over to the ice rink, Shelby had been irritated by the fact that no parking place had been reserved for him close to the judges' stand, and he'd had to park a hundred yards away. He was just as happy now as he drove the Cadillac out and headed for the hotel.

From what he could see, the hotel was a

total loss. He just hoped there hadn't been too many people in it when the avalanche hit. At the back, the snow appeared to be piled up about twenty feet—to the bottom of the third floor—and the whole building was tilting from the impact.

He parked by the front steps and hurried into the lobby. The place was a shambles. The ceiling was sagging and broken in a few places, and the floor was buckled and strewn with plaster and broken glass. At the rear, and covering the entrance to the dining room, a solid mass of snow and ice was sloping in as far as the registration desk. The place was also dark, and he almost knocked Susan off her feet as he collided with her coming the other way. He quickly grabbed her arm.

"What's going on?"

"The power's out," she said when she recognized him. "There was an explosion in the kitchen, and everyone in the dining room is trapped."

"Do you know how many are in there?"

"No, but I'm sure there must have been a few people."

Shelby looked at the mass of snow covering the door. "We'll probably have to dig into it from the outside."

"Some men are out there trying it right now."

"Good. Have you seen my mother?"

"No. But, David, there's gas leaking out of the kitchen again. Maybe into the dining room."

"Oh, Christ!" He headed toward the offices in the east wing, then shouted back,

"Baby, get someone to help you. Get all the blankets and sheets you can carry and take them to the ice rink. Fast! There's a lot of people hurt down there."

The whole corridor was tilted and the floor was covered with fragments of plaster. He hesitated a moment, then found the door to the telephone-switchboard room.

"Has anyone got through to Cedar Falls?" he asked in the darkness. Then he stopped abruptly.

The switchboard was no longer against the wall. The whole thing was angled crazily on the floor, and two men were trying to lift it from the operator's inert body. Shelby quickly grabbed a corner and hoisted.

The girl was unconscious, but still alive. "Get a stretcher or something and get her out of here. And see if you can make that switchboard work. Steve," he said, finally recognizing one of the men, "take whoever you need, get into SkiHaven, and work on the back-up generator."

Shelby continued down the corridor and then outside, where he could make his way around to the dining room. As he climbed over the snow he glanced up at the back of the building. Every window in the place was broken—probably from the building having twisted with the impact. But at least the people up there could get out.

About eight men were digging into the packed snow behind the dining room, some of them using picks to break up the ice slabs. Phil Prentiss was directing the operation. He shook his head when he saw Shelby.

"I don't know, David, it's slow going. And I don't think we can get any power equipment in here."

Shelby watched the men dig for a minute, seeing the hopelessness of it. "You got any dynamite?"

"Yeah, out in the truck."

"Go get it."

Shelby stared at the building, wondering how many people might be trapped in there. Most of the guests had probably been at the ski lift or the ice rink. But there were bound to be some who were having a late breakfast.

Prentiss had a worried look when he came back with the dynamite. "If we blast too close, we may cave in the whole place."

"And if we don't get to them fast, they'll asphyxiate. Susan said there was gas still leaking in there."

Prentiss nodded and gave him a grim look. "What do you want to do?"

Shelby took a deep breath and tried to imagine the people trapped inside, and how they would feel about it. If it were him, he would want his rescuers to take any kind of risk to get them out as quickly as possible. "Blast," he said.

The gas had a sickeningly sweet odor to it. Mrs. Shelby brought the last of the curtains to McDade, and he squeezed them into the crevices where he had stacked tables around the door to the kitchen.

"You think that's really going to do any good?" Mrs. Shelby asked.

McDade shook his head and glanced at

the ceiling. "It may stop some of it. But I think it's coming through that cracked plaster, too."

"God, I wish I could have a cigarette." Mrs. Shelby sighed. She picked up a chair and suddenly threw it across the room toward the snow.

"That won't do any good, Mrs. Shelby," McDade said wearily.

"The name's Florence, dammit! And I won't just sit here, McDade."

Caroline trudged down the road, her hands deep in the pockets of her parka as she stared up at the mountainside. It was still mostly white, but there were now streaks of rock and earth visible in places. Lower down on the slopes, whole groves of pine trees had been up-rooted and swept down, leaving deep scars of dirt visible through the white. She wouldn't have believed that much snow could slide off a mountain.

Ahead of her, one of the slides had come down to within a few feet of the road and formed a thick bank of snow that was hanging over a gully. She gazed curiously at it for a minute, then stopped walking. What she had thought was a broken tree branch sticking from the snowbank had a mitten on the end of it.

She finally moved forward, feeling a little sick as she made out the forearm and elbow. Then she saw the red stains in the snow next to it. She climbed up the snowbank, knowing she should check the pulse and see if the person was still alive. She reached for the wrist, then jumped back as a loud horn suddenly blasted just behind her.

"What's the matter, lady?" a man called out.

It was a big television truck with the words MARK ELLIOT SHOW painted on the side. Caroline stared at the man, then looked back at the arm.

"Jeeesus!" the truck driver said when he saw it. "How far is it to the hotel, lady?"

"I don't know. Just go—"

"Come on, get in! I'll give you a lift."

Caroline moved slowly down the embankment and around the truck, taking one last glance at the arm. The person had to be dead, she told herself.

"Jeez, what's going on around here?" the man asked when she got in. "Cars have been roaring down this road like the world's coming to an end. Is that guy dead back there?"

"I think so. There's been an avalanche."

"Oh yeah?" The man turned and shouted through a window in the back of the cab. "D'ja hear that, Freddie? And we missed it!"

The first charge of dynamite blasted out six feet of snow and loosened enough so that they could easily dig out another two or three feet. But there was still another ten or twelve feet packed against the building. Shelby looked it over and climbed out of the hole.

"A couple more, I think, Phil. Then we'll have to dig the rest."

Prentiss jumped in the hole with a crowbar and started gouging out a niche for the dynamite. Shelby watched him for a minute, then glanced to the side as someone climbed over the snow toward them.

"Caroline!" He hurried over and helped her down the slope.

"There was no word on the news," she said. "The radio went dead."

"I know. We're cut off. Was my mother with you?"

"No, I haven't seen her."

Shelby looked at her, about to ask where she had been when the avalanche hit. Then he decided against it.

"David, hand me the sticks," Prentiss said from the hole.

10

◇◇◇◇◇◇◇◇◇◇◇◇◇◇◇◇◇◇◇◇◇◇◇◇◇◇◇◇◇◇◇◇◇◇◇◇

The driver kept the big truck in low gear as he moved along the slippery road. The woman had said the ski lift was about a mile farther on, and he searched the landscape trying to spot some kind of building in all the whiteness. Freddie, the technical director, had moved up front with him and was watching also.

It was incredible how much tumbled snow and debris were spread across the bottom of the valley. Sirens were wailing somewhere, but there were no fire trucks or ambulances in sight.

"That must be it," Freddie finally said. "Over there where those cars are parked."

"Jeez, what a mess," the driver said. Half the cars were buried under ten feet of snow. The building that must have housed the ski-lift machinery was flat on the ground with a bunch of tangled wires and cables coming out of the snow.

He pulled the truck in as close as he could, and all the crew members piled out. Stan Hayden, the director, led them across the snow to where three skiers were hurriedly attaching equipment and coils of rope to their belts.

"What's going on, pal?" Hayden asked.

"There's a man and a kid hanging from the ski-lift cables up there." The skier tightened his belt a notch and yelled at the others, "Let's go."

Hayden pulled out a pocket telescope and focused it on the slope, following the tangle of cables a quarter of a mile up the side of the mountain.

"Holy Christ!" he said. A man was dangling in the air about sixty feet above the slope, a little kid hanging on his back. "Look at that, Freddie," he said, and handed over the telescope.

"My God," Freddie gasped. He lowered the glass. "What can we do?"

"What else? Set up." Hayden headed back to the truck.

"What?" Freddie exclaimed.

"Shoot. Come on, move your ass. Let's get the cameras!"

Holy Christ, Freddie thought as he followed; if his own mother was having a heart attack, Stanley Hayden would run for his camera. And when he got it, he would probably pinch the poor woman to get her to show more pain on her face.

The five men hauled out the equipment and followed Hayden to a high mound of snow where they had a clear view of everything. The camera operator set up his tripod and an assistant fixed up a screen to protect it from the light snow that had begun to fall. Then he waved down at the van with the generator.

"Okay," Hayden said, "get a quick establishing shot of the mountains, then zoom in on the guy and the kid on the cable. And stick with 'em, for Crissake. If they fall, we don't want to miss it."

"Yes, sir," Freddie said.

Mark Elliot no longer had any feeling in his hands. By sheer will alone he kept them closed on the steel shaft, but he didn't dare move his head.

"There's more of them coming, Mr. Elliot," Jason said with a hopeful note in his voice.

"Try not to move too much, Jason." Elliot's arms felt like frozen chunks of lead, and his nose and ears were now frostbitten. He wasn't sure he could last much longer. "What are they doing down there?"

"I don't know. It looks like they're getting out some ropes or something."

Oh, God, let it be a net, Elliot prayed.

"Hang on up there!" somebody shouted from below.

It seemed hopeless, but the ski patrolmen moved methodically across the slope searching for blood or pieces of clothing or fragments of skis—anything that might suggest the presence of a buried body. At any indication, they stopped and the two men with avalanche probes forced the long rods down into the snow. Occasionally they hit something, and those with shovels dug furiously. Sometimes it would be a plank or a broken tree branch, sometimes a body.

Of the twenty or so people they had found, half of them had been dead. The others were taken down the slope in rescue baskets and were lined up near the parking lot to be given whatever first aid was available.

Annette did what she could. Blankets had been brought from the hotel, and she covered the survivors as they were brought down. Then she tried to comfort them.

When more blankets arrived, she grabbed a handful and headed up the slope. One of the ski patrolmen had asked for them, and she was anxious to see if there was any sign of Bruce up there.

Several other people were climbing the slope now, bringing shovels to help with the digging. She followed what had become a beaten path in the soft snow, then looked around after she had delivered the blankets.

"Have you seen Bruce Scott anywhere around?" she asked a passing patrolman.

The man shook his head. "He was making his run when the avalanche hit." He skied off to where several volunteers were bringing a body from a hole.

Annette watched, but it was not Bruce. She climbed higher on the slope, to the area the patrolmen had already searched, then moved off in the other direction. It seemed hopeless. There were acres and acres of tumbled snow, and parts of it must be at least forty feet deep. Was it even possible for him to still be alive?

She scanned the snow in all directions and then headed down again, starting miniature avalanches as the snow broke away beneath her. Then she stumbled and slid twenty feet before the soft snow stopped her. She got to her feet and brushed herself off, then glanced back at the long trough her body had made. Then she froze, staring at the speck of red near the top. Was it blood?

She quickly scrambled up the snow, slipping and sliding as it gave way beneath her. The red spot was not blood. It was wool yarn! She quickly pulled it out and brushed the frozen snow away. It was a red cap with a bright yellow stripe. It was Bruce's!

"Help!" she cried. "Over here! Bruce is under here somewhere!"

She dug with her hands, throwing snow in all directions as the three patrolmen quickly came.

"Take it easy, lady," one of them said. "Let's find out exactly where he is first."

The man with the probe eased it in directly below the spot where she'd found the cap. Then slowly and methodically he thrust the probe into more spots, making a spiral pattern away from the cap. He found no resistance. The others watched and waited with their shovels.

About twenty feet below the spot, he finally hit something. "About four feet down," he said as the other men hurried down and dug.

When they reached the body, they used their hands, and then gently lifted the man

149

from the hole and turned him over. Annette stared and then felt her heart sink as she saw the face.

"Bruce . . ." the man said weakly.

It was Bruce's coach. He was wearing the same red jacket with the yellow stripe.

A hundred yards higher on the slope, Bruce Scott could no longer feel his hands or feet, and he had given up digging at the hard snow. He breathed shallowly, his eyes closed, and a pleasant drowsiness was now engulfing him. "Can you hear me?" he called out weakly.

"It's getting worse," McDade said. He lifted his head from his knees and took a deep breath, trying to fight off the nausea.

Mrs. Shelby stopped digging and looked at him, suddenly feeling faint herself. The gas was making her throat dry. More than anything else, she wished she had a drink. Why hadn't they been trapped in one of the cocktail lounges instead of the dining room?

"There's no point in digging anymore, Mrs. Shelby."

"Florence," she said hoarsely.

McDade nodded. "Florence."

He was right about the digging. They hadn't even made a dent in the snow. She pulled herself to her feet and moved unsteadily across the room. "When you've got to go, McDade," she said with an odd smile, "you might as well make it a snappy ending."

McDade stared at her and at the doorway they had tried to seal with curtains. To his relief, she didn't go to the door, but plopped herself down on the piano bench. She sat silently for a minute, as if thinking about something. Then she banged out a couple of chords and lifted her head. "If you were the only boy in the world," she sang in a rasping voice, "and I were the only girl . . ."

The explosion lifted McDade three inches off the floor. Across the room, the piano jumped, and Mrs. Shelby was suddenly on her back instead of sitting on the bench.

More plaster cascaded from the ceiling, and for a minute McDade couldn't see her across the room. He crawled a few paces, then rose and felt his way to her.

"Mrs. Shelby . . . Florence? Are you all right?"

She was up on an elbow, frowning at the snow. "Jesus Christ, did I bring the house down again?"

"I think they're dynamiting the snow from the outside. That must be what we heard a little earlier."

She eased her head back and closed her eyes, suddenly looking exhausted. McDade moved closer and looked up at the buckled ceiling. The hissing of gas seemed louder now, as if the second explosion had opened the pipe farther. He looked over at Mrs. Shelby, but she didn't seem to be aware of it.

"How close to the wall can you get us, Phil?" Shelby asked. The men were hurriedly clearing away the loose snow now.

"To within five or six feet of the wall. Do

you know how much pressure it can take?"

"It was built to withstand hundred-mile-an-hour winds."

Prentiss nodded and began bundling more dynamite sticks together.

"Harvey," Shelby said to one of the waiters, "go and round up everybody you can find and bring all the sharp-edged tools you can lay your hands on." He turned back to Prentiss. "You open it up, and I'll get us through the glass."

Inside, McDade managed to bring over two tables to shield them from any further blasts. When he finally squeezed in behind them with Mrs. Shelby, he gazed woozily at her for a minute before he realized how gray her face had become. He reached over and touched her cheek, then gently shook her.

"Florence?"

She mumbled something, and her head drooped to the side.

She needed oxygen—artificial respiration. But McDade was too weak to give it to her. And there probably wasn't enough oxygen in his breath to do her any good anyway. He gently took her hand in both of his, then rested his head against the wall. He felt her squeeze his fingers for a moment. At least there was still a little life in her.

Suddenly the floor jumped again. Another deluge of dust and plaster rained down on them. McDade closed his eyes and dropped his head for a minute. Then he looked across the room.

In the snow behind the window there was a large crack, and there seemed to be some faint light coming from it. Or was he imagining things?

"Florence?" McDade said. He got a hand under her arm and tried to lift her, but he didn't have the strength. When he eased back again her head dropped gently into his lap.

Using a broad-mouthed shovel, Shelby scooped the last of the debris aside. Then he saw the ten-inch fissure at the bottom of the pit. He quickly grabbed a smaller shovel from one of the waiters and gouged out a foot-and-a-half-wide tunnel. He finally heard the clank of steel against glass. Then he squeezed in, thrusting forward the small flashlight Prentiss handed him.

He could see nothing at first. The glass was wet and frosted with snow. Behind it there seemed to be nothing but empty space. He pulled a handkerchief from his pocket and wiped the glass, then peered in again.

He could see nothing but tumbled furniture and rubble at first. If anyone was in there, they were either dead or unconscious. Then, behind a toppled table he finally saw the huddled form against the far wall. It was a man, and he was alive. He was lifting his head and gazing feebly across at the window.

"My God," Shelby breathed. It was McDade! And the woman he was cradling in his arms was his mother!

From inside, McDade squinted uncertainly at the pinpoint of light. He had to do something, he told himself. If he didn't, neither he nor Mrs. Shelby would last much longer.

He gently lifted Mrs. Shelby's head from his lap and slid out from under her. His hands were too numb to feel anything now, but he picked up a heavy chair and moved unsteadily forward. Mustering all the strength he had left, he lunged forward and heaved his weight against the chair, slamming the legs into the glass.

"McDade!" Shelby yelled as soon as the splintered fragments crashed to the floor. He quickly wriggled forward and squeezed through the tunnel. Inside, he rolled McDade to his back.

"Prentiss! Hurry!" Shelby called through the tunnel. He dragged McDade closer to the hole, and Prentiss pulled him through.

The sickeningly sweet odor of gas made Shelby gag as he hurried across to his mother. She was staring vacantly into space when he picked her up and stumbled back.

Outside, Caroline held her breath as she watched Prentiss drag McDade from the narrow tunnel. Then she felt a wave of relief as McDade opened his eyes and blinked woozily. Three other men quickly jumped into the pit and helped carry him out.

Prentiss returned to the tunnel, and a moment later he was backing out, pulling Mrs. Shelby along by the shoulders. Then David was coming through.

Caroline felt her heart sink as she watched them bring Mrs. Shelby out of the pit. She appeared to be dead. Her face was grayish-blue, and her arms dropped limply as they laid her down on the snow. Caroline grabbed some blankets and quickly covered her.

"Is she breathing?"

Shelby leaned over and held his ear close to her mouth. He finally straightened, a look of anguish on his face. "I don't think so."

Bruce Scott gazed dully at the pattern of snow crystals six inches from his face. In the gray darkness they took on all sorts of different forms. Sometimes they looked like huge caverns, large enough for a man to walk into. Then they looked like a blurry landscape, a treacherous slope where he would have to be careful picking his course. Then a huge drop of water formed from the condensation of his breath. It hung for a moment just above his nose, then dropped and trickled into his eye.

"Can anybody hear me?" he pleaded in a hoarse whisper.

He was going to die, he had finally decided.

He closed his eyes, and his thoughts drifted aimlessly back to a warm day in Sun Valley, Idaho. He was fifteen years old and it was his first competitive slalom race. He was a scrawny kid with acne who was permitted to compete only because one of the other entries had broken his leg the day before.

He had skied with complete abandon that day, knowing the others were stronger and far more experienced than he. But he had never skied better, and when his time was announced and he had run the course two and a half seconds faster than any of the others, the judges had all conferred for five minutes making certain the clocks had not malfunctioned. And then he had stood on the winner's stand, grinning and crying at the same time while the judge put the ribbon and gold medal around his neck.

That night a twenty-nine-year-old woman named Mrs. Carlyle took him to her room and gave him his first taste of champagne. Then she had quietly stripped off all his clothing and knelt before him, saying that he had a wonderful career ahead of him and that he should enjoy it to the fullest.

Bruce smiled faintly as he remembered that night. It was his first experience with a woman, and of all those he'd had since, none of them had been quite the same. And none of the hundreds of medals he had won since had given him quite the thrill he'd experienced that day in Sun Valley.

He didn't want to die.

"Can anybody hear me?" he whimpered almost inaudibly.

Just to the left of his face a chunk of snow broke away and wedged tightly against his ear. He tried to turn his head away from it. He finally drew his hand closer and scraped at it, but it seemed to press harder, forcing some of the snow into his ear.

Then he felt it, the movement of metal sliding down next to his head. Within the confined area, he twisted as far to the right as he could. Then he saw the metal moving steadily upward.

"Help!" he cried out, at the same time

grabbing at the slender probe. His numbed hand seemed to go off in the wrong direction, and he grabbed again, once more screaming as loudly as he could.

For an instant he had it. His fingers were around it, but they would not close on it. Then it was gone, disappearing into the neat little hole just above his face.

"Oh, God, help me," he whimpered. The effort to grab the metal rod seemed to have exhausted the last of his strength.

High above him, the ski patrolman drew up the probe as fast as he could, at the same time noting its length. "Over here!" he shouted to the men with the shovels.

The men moved quickly, and a couple others glided across on skis.

"Someone's buried pretty deep," the man said. "About thirty feet down." He had the probe all the way out now, and he frowned at the bloody tip as he folded it. "And he's bleeding."

"Get that plow over here!" one of the men on skis shouted.

Annette moved quickly across the slope with her coach. "It might be Bruce."

"Don't get your hopes up."

Her coach watched as Annette picked up a shovel and dug furiously into the packed snow.

Caroline counted slowly, then took another deep breath and placed her mouth over Mrs. Shelby's. With her right hand just below Florence's breastbone, she felt the air entering the lungs. Then there was a faint vibration that might have been a heartbeat.

Around her, the men were all silent, waiting hopefully. David rubbed his mother's hand, trying to warm it.

"An ambulance just pulled up in front, Mr. Shelby," one of the waiters announced.

"Thank God! Get 'em back here fast!"

Caroline lifted her head an inch and listened at Mrs. Shelby's mouth. "I think she's breathing." She picked up the other hand and massaged it. Mrs. Shelby's eyelids fluttered for an instant.

The two ambulance attendants came over the snow with a stretcher. When they arrived, the first man dropped to his knees and clamped a plastic oxygen mask over Mrs. Shelby's face and checked her pulse.

He finally smiled as several men stepped forward and transferred her to the stretcher. "I think she's going to be fine. You did a good job, miss," he said to Caroline.

"Thank God," Shelby breathed.

Four men gripped the stretcher and moved across the snow.

Off to the side, McDade had vomited. When he saw Mrs. Shelby being carried away, he quickly rose and followed the procession to the front of the hotel.

"Now, you behave," he said to her at the ambulance.

She lifted the oxygen mask and gave him a wry smile. "Get out of here, McDade," she said hoarsely.

"Henry," he corrected her.

"Please, sir," the attendant said as they rolled her in.

Caroline got in beside her, and Shelby leaned in. "Mom?"

"It's all right, Mr. Shelby," the attendant told him, "she'll be okay now."

Mrs. Shelby gave them all a sour look and pushed the mask aside again. "I don't want this. I want a Bloody Mary."

Caroline smiled as they closed the door. "It's all right, David."

Shelby watched as the big car pulled away. A second ambulance was coming along from the ski-lift area, and fell in behind as they headed down the mountain.

The snow was falling heavily now, and the mountains were no longer visible. Shelby watched as more bodies were being brought from behind the hotel. Then he turned to the fire captain. "Charley, can you get me out to the lift?"

"Sure thing, Mr. Shelby."

Nick Thorne delivered his twelfth body to the parking lot of the ice rink. This one was dead—a man about sixty whose neck apparently had been broken with the first impact. The sad part of it was, in his gloved right hand he was holding the fingers of an empty mitten, as if in the last minute he was trying to save somebody—or maybe share the final moment of life.

As Nick stretched out the body, Shelby's

159

secretary, Susan, hurried over with a blanket. Nick shook his head, letting her know there was no rush.

It was amazing, he thought as he headed up the slope again. Some of the people he would have expected to panic and fall apart completely in a crisis had shown nothing but courage and selflessness. Shelby's secretary was one of them. Since the minute she arrived at the ice rink with a load of blankets, she had been going at full speed, comforting survivors and doing whatever else was necessary to keep things organized.

Nick returned to the same spot where he had found the dead man. A short distance away he had seen a shadow two or three feet below the surface, and now he dug carefully with the shovel. Then he dropped to his knees and scooped away the snow with his hands.

An arm came into view, and he hesitated as the hand suddenly moved and lifted from the snow. The nails were painted a silvery pink, and on one of the fingers was a huge star-sapphire ring. Below that, falling close to the elbow, a diamond bracelet was crusted with snow.

Nick dug toward the head and suddenly found an earring with a sapphire that matched the ring. He looked at it for a minute, then placed it in the woman's waiting hand.

11

◇◇◇◇◇◇◇◇◇◇◇◇◇◇◇◇◇◇◇◇◇◇◇◇◇◇◇◇◇◇

It seemed to be taking them forever to get to
Bruce. When the snowplow came, they couldn't
go directly over the area for fear of crushing
him under the weight, and they had churned
out a deep cut just below him on the slope.
Then four men had gone in with shovels, and
finally one man was tunneling down by himself.

Annette knew it had to be Bruce. He had
been the only person to ski down, and no one
else would have had any reason to be that high
on the slope. Her coach put his arm around
her as they waited.

They could see only the ski patrolman's
boots now as he tunneled deeper. Then Annette
stiffened as the man suddenly quit digging.

"It looks like he's upside down," the man
called out. "I can feel his boots and one of his
legs."

He dug some more, then wriggled out.
"Somebody give me a rope. He's just about free

161

now, and we can slide him out with a line around his legs."

A man came forward with a coil of nylon rope, and the patrolman wriggled into the tunnel again. Annette put her hands over her eyes and took a deep breath. For some reason she had an ominous feeling about what was going to happen. If the man was dead, please have him be someone else, she prayed.

The patrolman edged out a little and then worked with the rope, straightening the legs. "Okay, take it slow," he said to the man behind.

The boots were too thick with snow for Annette to recognize them. But then she gasped and held her breath as the red ski pants became visible. Then the red parka with the yellow stripe. Then the face. It was Bruce!

Annette stared at the bloodstained face and the torn fingers on the curled hand. His eyes were partially open, but they were staring lifelessly out at nothing.

"Dead," one of the ski patrolmen said quietly.

Annette dropped slowly to her knees and felt herself trembling uncontrollably as she closed her eyes. "He was alive!" she whimpered. "He was alive! He was so alive!"

It was snowing so heavily now, Mark Elliot could no longer see the slope beneath them. Occasionally he could hear shouts, but he had no idea what the people were saying.

"Jason," he said, his own voice sounding strangely thick. "I'm going to try to go up this shaft. Do you think you can hang on a while longer?"

He could feel Jason shivering. The boy's breath was coming fast, as if he were feverish. "I think so," he answered.

One at a time, Elliot moved his fingers, trying to get some blood circulating in them again. Then he swung his legs in an effort to find the chair that he knew was dangling under them. He hit it with one foot and then the other, but there seemed to be nothing more than a vertical bar—nothing he could use for support.

"Hold on, Jason," he grunted. He raised both knees and lifted his feet as high as he could, groping for something—anything. He hit something hard, but his boots quickly slipped away. He tried again, this time lifting only one leg.

He had it! His knee was over the curve of an iron bar. It was slippery, but it was enough to give him a little support and take the pressure off his arms.

"Okay, Jason. Now I'm going to try to go up a little. Hang on."

His hands felt a little warmer now, and he wondered if it was the false warmth that came with frostbite. But with the support from below he could now free one hand, and he stuck it inside his parka for a minute. He did the same with the other hand and then reached higher, pulling himself and Mark a foot higher than the end of the shaft.

He could not lift his legs and get both feet on the curved iron bar. It was slippery as hell, and he didn't dare release his grip on the higher shaft. But it allowed him to stand almost straight up. From there he could nearly reach the sagging cable overhead.

He stretched out as far as possible, but he could get no more than his fingertips over the cable. He tried with the other hand, but he still couldn't reach.

He was no longer able to see it very well through the swirling snowflakes, but he knew the tower was only fifty or sixty feet down the cable. If he got to it, they could probably climb down. Or at worst they'd have something stable to hang onto. He looked up at the cable again, wondering. If he put all his weight on one foot, would he be able to stretch farther? It was worth a try.

He reached as high as he could on the shaft, lifted one foot from the curved bar, and stretched himself to the limit.

He had it! His fingers were around the cable, and he almost had it in his grip.

He was shifting the hand, trying to get another inch under his fingers, when Jason suddenly screamed. At the same time Elliot felt the iron bar drop out from beneath his foot.

With the chair breaking loose, and its weight suddenly gone, the cable snapped a foot higher, and for a moment they bounced and swung. But he still had one hand on the cable and the other on the steel shaft. "It's all right, Jason!" he said quickly.

He waited until they were no longer swinging. Then with one quick movement he brought his other hand over to the cable.

His hands were now torn, and rivulets of blood were running down his wrists. He stared at them for a minute, then inched his hands closer together. He took a long breath and rested for a minute. Then, moving a few inches at a time, he started working his way toward the lower tower.

The fire captain squeezed the big truck past as many cars as he could, then parked it just behind the television van.

Stanley Hayden was standing at the rear of the van. "You'll never get that fire truck up there," he said as Shelby jumped down.

"How are they doing?" Shelby asked.

"You're Shelby, aren't you?"

"That's right."

"Well, you can't see anything from here, but I've got a man with a mini-camera up there. You can take a look on the monitor if you want."

Shelby followed the man inside the van, where there were six monitor screens glowing. "Up there," Hayden said.

Shelby could see nothing more than a shadow in the white blur. Then the snow swirled away for a moment and he could see Mark Elliot hanging from the cable with a small boy clinging to his back. They were motionless for three or four seconds. Then Elliot shifted a hand, and they moved about three inches.

"He'll never make it," Hayden said.

While Shelby stared at the picture, another snow flurry turned it pure white. "How much of a drop is it?"

"Sixty or seventy feet. You got any idea who the guy is?"

Shelby gave him a startled look. "Don't you know? It's Mark Elliot."

The two technicians turned and frowned, and Hayden gaped at him. "That's Mark up there? You're kidding!"

Shelby headed for the steps. "That's what the fire captain told me."

"Holy Christ!" Hayden said behind him. "Jesus, what a show this is going to make! Don't lose those tapes, you guys!"

Shelby found the fire captain helping his men get out stretchers. "Charley, have you got a net on this truck?"

"Yeah."

"Get it out. Fast!" Shelby moved past the truck and spotted a ski patrolman climbing into a snowcat. "Hey! Bring that cat over here. On the double!"

Suddenly a man with a mini-camera rushed over and focused it on Shelby as he hurried back to the fire truck.

"Get the hell out of here!" Shelby roared.

"Mr. Elliot!" a raspy, amplified voice called out from somewhere below.

Elliot took a firm grip on the cable and held himself still, listening.

"We're bringing up a net, Mr. Elliot. Don't try to go any farther. Just remain still and try to save your strength. The snowcat's coming up with it right now!"

Thank God, Elliot thought. In the past five minutes he had moved only nine or ten feet, and his hands felt like there was nothing left but stripped bones.

"You all right, Jason?"

"Yes," the feeble voice answered.

Elliot could hear the engine of the snow-cat. A minute later it stopped, and somebody was shouting out orders. Elliot closed his eyes and felt his arms beginning to tremble as he held himself still. The icy wind was now penetrating to the bone, and his nose and ears were frozen. Hurry, dammit, he silently urged the men below.

"Mr. Elliot!" the rasping voice called again. "We're ready now, but you're going to have to come down one at a time. Can you get the boy to jump?"

"Did you hear that, Jason?" Elliot asked.

"Yes," the boy murmured.

"There's nothing to be afraid of, Jason. The worst part is letting go. After that, it'll take about two seconds. Then it will be like landing in a big soft pillow."

Jason whimpered an unintelligible protest.

"It's the only way, Jason. Much safer than staying up here. And I'm really tired of staying up here. Aren't you?"

Jason murmured something that sounded like agreement.

"All you have to do is close your eyes and let go. Pretend you're jumping into a nice warm swimming pool." He waited, but there was no sound or movement from the boy. "Jason, you've got to do it. Okay?"

He could feel the boy twisting to look down.

"Don't look, Jason. Just close your eyes and let go. I'll count to five. Okay?" Elliot closed his eyes for a minute and clenched his jaw. The cable was now cutting deeply into the flesh of his hands, scraping at the bone. "Okay, Jason. Here we go. One . . . two . . . three . . ."

Elliot felt the boy's arm slip away from his neck. Then a great weight seemed to fly from his body and Jason was gone. Elliot grimaced as the cable bounced, cracking more flesh on his hands.

From below, David Shelby held his breath as he saw the shadowy figure detach itself from the larger one and come plummeting downward. For an instant he could hear a soft cry from the boy and then he thudded squarely into the center of the net.

Shelby moved quickly forward and got a grip under the boy's arms. Someone else grabbed his feet, and they carried him off. One of the patrolmen was holding a blanket open, and they quickly wrapped him up.

"Get him down the hill fast," Shelby said. "He's probably suffering from frostbite."

The fireman with the bullhorn squinted up at the cable again. "Okay, Mr. Elliot! You can jump now!"

Shelby watched, but Elliot made no move. It was as if his hands were frozen to the cable and he was unable to free himself.

"You can jump now, Mr. Elliot," the fireman called out again.

Elliot's head was bent, as if he were studying the terrain and making certain the boy was out of the net and it was in the right position. Then one of his hands broke loose, and he made a half-turn, still dangling.

"Mr. Elliot, you . . ."

They all saw it coming—everyone except Mark Elliot. Off to the side and six feet above him, the other cable was swinging freely in the wind—a tangle of electrical conduit dangling a few feet under it. Just as the fireman shouted, the conduit seemed to spring uncoiled, and a broken ten-foot length of it whipped around and struck the lower cable. Sparks exploded in every direction. At the same time, Elliot's body seemed to twitch and contort, jumping like a puppet on wildly manipulated strings.

"Mark!" Shelby cried out.

Elliot's body jumped wildly in one final contortion. Then it was plummeting downward. The arms and legs were completely limp as it thudded into the snow ten feet down from the net.

"Oh, my God," Shelby groaned.

The firemen dropped the net and rushed down, but Shelby couldn't move.

He closed his eyes for a minute. Then he watched numbly as the firemen checked the body and slowly rose.

"He's dead," one of them said quietly.

Shelby helped them put the body in the snowcat. Then he trudged slowly down the slope. Somehow Mark's death made him feel guiltier than anything else. Mark was the only man he had ever trusted—the only man who

169

would ever tell him to his face that he was a damned fool. And he had killed him, just as surely as if he had held a gun to his head.

At the bottom, the TV director was standing next to the truck, his face drawn as he watched them lay the body next to the other corpses.

"Did you get a good picture?" Shelby asked.

The man stared at him for a minute. "Hey, don't pull that crap on me, fella. You're the guy who built this mountain paradise."

Shelby looked at him and walked on. The man was right, Shelby told himself. He was in no position to question other people's actions.

When the fire captain drove him back to the hotel, it seemed like the number of corpses lying out in front had doubled. Nick Thorne and Prentiss were just bringing a couple more over.

"How many?" Shelby asked.

Prentiss shook his head. "Don't know yet."

An ambulance turned the corner and came slowly into the parking lot, its lights flashing. Shelby stared at it, realizing it was the same ambulance that had followed his mother's down.

"What happened?" he asked the driver when it came to a stop.

The man stepped out and shook his head. "There were secondary slides all along the way. We got cut off from the other unit."

"You mean the ambulance with Mrs. Shelby?"

"Yes, sir. We had to turn back. I just talked to them over in SkiHaven and told them to send some plows down."

"Do you know if the other ambulance got through?"

"The last I talked to them on the radio, they were headed for the bridge."

Shelby frowned, wondering, then glanced over at Nick. "You got a car?"

"My jeep's over there."

"No, Florence," Caroline said, "they don't have mixings for a Bloody Mary in the ambulance."

Mrs. Shelby lifted the oxygen mask again. "They ought to, you know. Tomato juice is packed with vitamin C."

Caroline smiled and pressed the mask down again. Then she looked past the driver and through the windshield, her smile quickly fading. She could make out the bridge up ahead, but they were slipping and sliding in the fresh snow and the driver was fighting to keep them on the road.

The second ambulance had turned back about ten minutes ago, the driver had told her. Both of them had been lucky they hadn't ended up at the bottom of a ravine. They were about two hundred yards apart when the slide came roaring down the steep embankment without any warning. Their ambulance had been struck in the back by the edge of the slide, but the driver had the presence of mind to push the throttle to the floor, and they had fishtailed out of it. Apparently the ambulance in back had been just as fortunate and had stopped just in time. But the road was now covered with ten feet of snow.

Caroline watched as the driver slowed almost to a stop before he made the sharp turn onto the bridge. Then he leaned forward, squinting through the frosted window and the banging windshield wipers. He shook his head for a minute and glanced in the rearview mirror. Then his eyes widened. "Oh, my God," he cried.

Caroline quickly looked out the rear windows, and her heart jumped into her throat. The whole mountainside seemed to be crashing down, and huge boulders of snow were exploding and bounding along the bridge behind them.

The ambulance seemed to jump as the driver stepped on the gas. But then the back wheels were spinning and for an instant they were sideways on the bridge. Then they were being hurtled in every direction.

Caroline grabbed for the side, groping for anything to give her support. For an instant she was gripping a handle; then the door suddenly flew open and she was tumbling out and skidding along the icy surface of the bridge.

She had no idea how she got there, but an instant later she was clinging desperately to a railing post of the bridge, and she could hear the thunderous roar of ice and snow crashing down into the ravine. Then she gasped, horrified as she saw the underside of the ambulance far below her. The big car spun in midair for an instant, and then it was bouncing and tumbling into the pit of the canyon.

For a moment there was silence. Then Caroline stared across to the other end of the bridge as great chunks of ice and snow began tumbling down from the slope above it. A moment later the whole mountainside seemed to roar downward in one piece. With a sudden wrenching sound the far end of the bridge broke loose from the mountain and went plunging downward.

The railing Caroline was clinging to was dropping and swinging to the side. She closed her eyes and ducked her head, waiting for the long plunge to her death. But just as suddenly as it had started moving, the railing let out a loud metallic screech and came to a stop.

Caroline lifted her head. She was not dead yet. But immediately below her there was nothing, and above, the railing and the segment of bridge she was clinging to were hanging from the mountain at a forty-five-degree angle.

Nick hesitated for only a moment when he reached the pile of snow blocking the road. He shoved the gear lever into low and angled up the side, slipping and fishtailing, sometimes sinking a little as they hit the softer spots. He managed to keep the jeep moving, and a minute later they bounced down to the road and were racing along at a good clip again.

With the heavy snowfall and dark clouds, it could just as well have been midnight for all that they could see. But Nick knew the road well, and he pushed it to full speed every chance he got.

They made the final broad curve into the mountain, and then the tight turn that led down the slope to the bridge. Nick leaned forward, watching closely now. Then he hit the brakes and they slid sideways into the bank of tumbled snow just before the entrance to the bridge.

"Oh, my God," Shelby groaned as the headlights beamed out over the empty chasm. They couldn't see the far side, but enough of the drooping wreckage was visible to make it apparent what had happened.

Nick had a dark feeling as they both got out and climbed the snowbank. A part of the bridge railing, along with a strip of the roadbed, was visible, all of it slanting sharply downward.

"They probably made it across before it happened," Nick said. He wasn't that confident, but he hoped it would give Shelby some hope.

Shelby nodded. He gazed emptily across the canyon for a minute. Then he took a deep breath, as if preparing himself for the worst, and moved slowly back toward the jeep.

"David?" Nick said. "Did you hear something?"

Shelby turned, and they both stood silently for a minute, listening. With no wind, and the snow coming down in big soft flakes, it seemed extraordinarily quiet. Then they heard it—a faint voice muffled by snowfall. They couldn't make out the words, but there was no doubt about the urgent tone.

"Where's it coming from?" Shelby asked.

They listened again, but the cry was no

more than a distant and muffled squeak in the darkness.

"Somebody must be on the broken part of the bridge," Nick said.

He moved quickly down the slope and back to the jeep. He pressed the horn button for a long four seconds and then grabbed a flashlight.

When he got back, Shelby was already making his way down to the bridge. Nick bounded down the soft snow, and they both stopped and listened again.

"Where are you?" Nick called out.

The voice answered, but they still couldn't make out the words or the direction from which they were coming. Nick switched on the flashlight and ran the beam slowly down what was left of the paved section of the bridge. They could see nothing but snow and the ragged edge where it had broken off.

"Look," Shelby said, "at the railing near the end."

Nick turned the light on the railing and moved it steadily downward. Then he saw his own bright blue parka and Caroline's desperate face looking up at them. She was clinging to a railing post, her boots hanging over the broken edge of the road.

"Caroline!" Shelby yelled, and moved quickly onto the bridge.

"David! Wait!"

Nick's warning came too late. Shelby's feet went out from under him the moment he stepped onto the sloping surface. For a moment he seemed to be all right, and he was groping for the railing. Then he slipped again, and he was suddenly gathering momentum as he raced downward. Nick held his breath for an instant, expecting both of them to go flying off the end. But Caroline held on tight when the collision came. Then Shelby grabbed the railing post just above hers.

"Hold on!" Nick yelled. He bounded up the slope as fast as he could and slid down the other side to the jeep. From the rear seat he grabbed a hundred-foot coil of rope and hurried back to the bridge.

The anchor post for the railing was still standing and vertical. He looped the rope around it twice and then tossed the coil down along the inside of the railing. It skittered down, and Shelby grabbed it with his free hand.

"Don't take any chances, David!" Nick yelled. "Loop it around both of your waists and secure it! Just take your time!"

Nick watched as Shelby worked carefully with the rope. Then he gazed into the ravine where the ambulance must have plunged. After a minute he saw a faint flickering of orange through the falling snow.

"Okay," Shelby finally shouted.

Nick braced himself, then pulled steadily on the rope, looping it around the anchor post as they made their way up.

12

◇◇◇◇◇◇◇◇◇◇◇◇◇◇◇◇◇◇◇◇◇◇◇◇◇◇◇◇◇◇◇◇

The sun was shining brightly the next morning. When she awakened, Caroline looked over at Nick's side of the bed, but the pillow was still smooth and the blankets were unruffled. She slid out of the bed and then grimaced from all the aches and pains as she put on a robe.

From the kitchen window she could see an army helicopter slowly descending near the hotel. Another one was lifting off, taking bodies away.

Caroline had worked until three in the morning, nursing the survivors, cooking, helping find accommodations for those whose rooms had been swept away. Then Nick had shoved his jeep keys into her hand and told her to go up to his cabin and get some sleep.

She thought about Tina Elliot as she ate breakfast. They had found her late that night when they were searching all the hotel rooms.

It looked as if she had taken the pills before the avalanche hit. But there was no note and no clear explanation of why she had done it.

Caroline wondered what caused women to behave as Tina did. Mark Elliot had probably been as kind and thoughtful as any husband could be. And as successful as he was, he was the kind of man most women dreamed of marrying. Maybe, in a little different way, Tina had suffered from the same lack of identification Caroline had felt when she was married to David. Her husband was famous and successful, and by setting out to get a superstar like Bruce Scott, she was trying to prove that she had some special talents of her own.

It was sad. Caroline wondered how many other housewives in the world secretly tried to paint, or write novels, or dreamed of getting recognition in some other way. And how many of them considered ending their frustrations the way Tina had.

The dead bodies of Cathy Jordan and her coach had also been found, and that seemed even sadder. And Gary Buckner had also died.

When she finished breakfast, Caroline cleaned up the dishes, then drove the jeep back to the hotel.

There were army trucks and bulldozers all over the place now. The area where the condominiums had been was being carefully cleared, a couple dozen soldiers searching the debris for more bodies. Behind the hotel the mountains looked beautiful. The snowfall during the night had covered all the ugly scars of the avalanches, and it once more looked like a Christmas card.

She parked the jeep and walked slowly up the steps, then paused for a minute. In the pile of snow-covered rubble at the side, the top of an unopened champagne bottle was protruding several inches. Caroline picked it up and smiled as Nick came through the front door.

"Nice and chilled," he said, glancing at the bottle.

He had a day's growth of whiskers, and his tired eyes showed that he hadn't gotten any sleep. "How is he?" Caroline asked.

"Okay. He's a fighter."

"Yes. Here's your keys. And thanks. I left your parka at the cabin."

"Anytime," he said, and smiled gently. "By the way, the army's opened the old road, and they're running convoys down every hour or so."

"Good. I'll sign up."

He nodded and gazed down at the steps as if looking for the right words to express something. "Caroline, I'm glad we met. It was very important to me. It was good to be reminded there are still some real human beings around."

Caroline smiled. "It was good for me too. But we're of different worlds, Nick."

"Yeah—that's true. And I like you the way you are."

There seemed to be nothing more to say. Nick smiled, looking as if he were going to fall asleep standing right there.

"Good-bye, Nick," she said, and moved up the steps.

David was standing at the side of the lobby where the registration desk used to be. He was still wearing his fur coat, but he looked almost comic with his stubbled chin and bloodshot eyes.

"Champagne?" Caroline asked.

Shelby blinked at her, then smiled. "Sure. What do you want to drink to?"

"Surviving."

"Yes, we have done that, haven't we?"

"Is there going to be a funeral for your mother?"

He shook his head. "No. She told me a long time ago she hated funerals and wanted no part of them. She said everybody should just have an extra drink the day after she died."

"A Bloody Mary, I presume."

He nodded and tore the foil off the champagne bottle. "I think she liked champagne just as well." He popped the cork and handed the bottle to Caroline.

"Cheers, Florence," she said, and took a drink.

"Cheers," Shelby said, and did the same.

"David, I think we've done more than survive. I thought I always knew you. But I really didn't. I'm looking at a man now that I really failed to see before."

He nodded. "It wasn't just you. I'm seeing it for the first time too." He looked around the hotel lobby and watched two soldiers carry a body out to the waiting trucks. "The responsibility is all mine. And I want it to be. Always."

Caroline looked at him, pleased with what she saw. Mostly she was pleased for his sake. "I love you, David," she said.

He smiled. "I know."

"And I have to be free."

"Yes, you do," he agreed.

She kissed him lightly on the stubbled cheek. Then she smiled and walked away. Her luggage was with a pile of bags in the corner. She picked up the two suitcases and paused at the front door.

He smiled and lifted the champagne bottle in salute as she walked out.

ABOUT THE AUTHOR

ROBERT WEVERKA was born in Los Angeles and educated at the University of Southern California, where he majored in economics. His other novels include: *Griff, Search, The Sting, Moonrock, The Widowed Master, One Minute to Eternity, Apple's Way, The Waltons, I Love My Wife,* and *March or Die.* He and his family currently live in Idyllwild, California.

READ YOUR WAY TO ADVENTURE

And share the joys and frustrations, triumphs and defeats of other young people.

RELAX!
SIT DOWN
and Catch Up On Your Reading!

☐	11877	HOLOCAUST by Gerald Green	$2.25
☐	11260	THE CHANCELLOR MANUSCRIPT by Robert Ludlum	$2.25
☐	10077	TRINITY by Leon Uris	$2.75
☐	2300	THE MONEYCHANGERS by Arthur Hailey	$1.95
☐	11266	THE MEDITERRANEAN CAPER by Clive Cussler	$1.95
☐	2500	THE EAGLE HAS LANDED by Jack Higgins	$1.95
☐	2600	RAGTIME by E. L. Doctorow	$2.25
☐	10888	RAISE THE TITANIC! by Clive Cussler	$2.25
☐	11966	THE ODESSA FILE by Frederick Forsyth	$2.25
☐	11770	ONCE IS NOT ENOUGH by Jacqueline Susann	$2.25
☐	11708	JAWS 2 by Hank Searls	$2.25
☐	8844	TINKER, TAILOR, SOLDIER, SPY by John Le Carre	$1.95
☐	11929	THE DOGS OF WAR by Frederick Forsyth	$2.25
☐	10526	INDIA ALLEN by Elizabeth B. Coker	$1.95
☐	10357	THE HARRAD EXPERIMENT by Robert Rimmer	$1.95
☐	10422	THE DEEP by Peter Benchley	$2.25
☐	10500	DOLORES by Jacqueline Susann	$1.95
☐	11601	THE LOVE MACHINE by Jacqueline Susann	$2.25
☐	10600	BURR by Gore Vidal	$2.25
☐	10857	THE DAY OF THE JACKAL by Frederick Forsyth	$1.95
☐	11952	DRAGONARD by Rupert Gilchrist	$1.95
☐	2491	ASPEN by Burt Hirschfeld	$1.95
☐	11330	THE BEGGARS ARE COMING by Mary Loos	$1.95

Buy them at your local bookstore or use this handy coupon for ordering:

Bantam Books, Inc., Dept. FBB, 414 East Golf Road, Des Plaines, Ill. 60016

Please send me the books I have checked above. I am enclosing $_____
(please add 50¢ to cover postage and handling). Send check or money order
—no cash or C.O.D.'s please.

Mr/Mrs/Miss_____

Address_____

City_____State/Zip_____

FBB—7/78

Please allow four weeks for delivery. This offer expires 1/79.

Bantam Book Catalog

Here's your up-to-the-minute listing of every book currently available from Bantam.

This easy-to-use catalog is divided into categories and contains over 1400 titles by your favorite authors.

So don't delay—take advantage of this special opportunity to increase your reading pleasure.

Just send us your name and address and 25¢ (to help defray postage and handling costs).

BANTAM BOOKS, INC.
Dept. FC, 414 East Golf Road, Des Plaines, Ill. 60016

Mr./Mrs./Miss_____
(please print)

Address_____

City_____State_____Zip_____

Do you know someone who enjoys books? Just give us their names and addresses and we'll send them a catalog too!

Mr./Mrs./Miss_____

Address_____

City_____State_____Zip_____

Mr./Mrs./Miss_____

Address_____

City_____State_____Zip_____

FC—6/77